WHAT SHE FOUND

MARTINA MONROE BOOK 6

H.K. CHRISTIE

KEEKSTAR
MEDIA

1

SADIE

How had we gotten here? When I first met Blaine, he swept me off my feet, and I was certain I'd found my prince charming. I was young and naïve then and didn't realize how difficult relationships and marriage could be. Everything started out great. We would take weekend trips to wine country or sail to Catalina Island and bask in the sunshine of the San Francisco Bay. As we held hands, walking carefree in the Presidio, admiring views of the Golden Gate Bridge, he made me feel like the luckiest woman on Earth.

It was during those trips that I would try to picture what my future children would be like. Would they look like me or Blaine? Maybe they would have my golden hair but Blaine's dark eyes and high cheekbones, sharp nose, and pointed chin. We were a young and healthy couple. Surely, we wouldn't have any problems creating our own little miracle.

Boy, had I been wrong. We married shortly after I turned thirty. Meaning we needed to get to work right away. After a year with no success, we visited a fertility specialist.

Sometimes I thought that was the beginning of the end. The end of the way things used to be. When our once passionate relationship turned clinical and mission-based, I should have known better. At first, Blaine was gung-ho and as a member of the medical community, knew that sometimes couples need a little extra help. He told me not to worry, that it would all work out. Flash forward four years — four heartbreaking years. It hadn't worked out.

He'd certainly handled it better than I did. But he wasn't the one who felt like a failure, month after month, as I stared at that stupid stick that was clearly out to get me. Each negative pregnancy result crushed me. How was it possible that I couldn't do on purpose what a lot of women had done on accident? It wasn't fair. I cursed my existence as I felt like less than a woman. Despite my accomplishments, my status in the community, and a successful marriage, I felt lost and unsure what the future would look like.

That was when Blaine started working late. He said that he needed to get in more clinical hours in the event he wanted to give up his family practice and switch over to working at a hospital. It meant he had two jobs, and I saw him less and less. Surely, that contributed to our lack of success in the baby-making department.

Over the last year, we had drifted apart, and he started acting peculiar. My best friend told me staying out late and not answering his cell phone when I called him were common signs of an affair. Talk about insult to injury. I searched for clues, determined to divorce that cheater if I found them, but I didn't look very hard. I loved Blaine and didn't want to lose him. All I wanted was our relationship to return to the way things were. Maybe it was just a phase we were going through? Maybe he wasn't really cheating? But he continued to stay out late, and my calls went to voicemail.

I had almost given up all hope until that morning.

The last year had been hard, dark, and depressing, but as I

placed my fingertips on my belly, I grinned. After all our hard work, our ups and our downs, our arguments, I nearly fainted when I saw that little plus sign. We had been on 'a break' from IVF and had relations only once in the last three months. It had been spontaneous after an entire bottle of wine. Was a bottle of Cabernet all I needed? That was silly. I knew that wasn't how these things worked and that some couples spent their life savings on IVF treatments and never had a successful pregnancy.

We were blessed, and I couldn't wait to tell Blaine. Deep down, I knew he was going to be thrilled and it would bring us back together — the way we used to be. And if he was having an affair, maybe this would be what would stop it. He would realize his family was the most important thing. Could I forgive his indiscretion? Yes. It had been a hard time for both of us. He worked too much, and I moped around when I wasn't also working.

As a surprise, I took the afternoon off from work and planned a romantic dinner on his boat to tell him the news. Blaine loved his boat — a mini yacht, really. So, I planned to sneak down to the boat and set up a romantic dinner with champagne and his favorite meal — chicken enchiladas and flan for dessert. Once out on the water, champagne flutes in hand, I would tell him he was going to be a father. We would embrace, kiss, and make love. I thought that night would change everything.

Before heading over to the marina, I hurried into the bathroom to check my reflection. It had been a while since I'd worn makeup, but for this special occasion, I pulled out rose-colored lipstick, rouge for my cheeks, and mascara to make my blue eyes sparkle. And to top it all off, I wore the dress he loved. It hugged my curves and put my cleavage on full display. He'd told me I drove him crazy when I wore it. Everything was just right.

With supplies in hand, I stepped out of our home and made my way to the driveway. I stopped and turned around to stare up at the house. It was a beautiful two-story that was too big for only two people. We would remedy that soon enough. Moving to the rear of my SUV, I popped the hatch and loaded the supplies.

On the drive to the marina, I contemplated all the different ways I could give Blaine our wonderful news. I thought maybe a note in his food or a baby booty next to his dinner plate. But I realized I didn't want to jinx it. It would be best to tell him when we were relaxed and cruising on the bay.

Parked at the marina, I lugged the cooler out to our slip. I set it down on the dock and stared out at the blue skies dotted with white, fluffy clouds. It was a perfect day.

My life was the fairytale I had wanted five years earlier when I married Blaine. He was a handsome and charming doctor, and I was a successful nurse, about to become a mother. We had a beautiful home in a beautiful neighborhood. We drove nice, new cars, and we never wanted for anything except for the baby, but as of that positive pregnancy test, we had that too. I pinched myself and giggled. This was my life. After worrying that my marriage was slipping away, I had everything I ever wanted.

On board, I trekked downstairs to the galley and unloaded dinner and beverages into the refrigerator. Turning toward the bow, I stopped. I thought I heard a muffled sound coming from the stateroom. My once-content smile melted.

Was it my imagination or had I heard something or someone?

Heart racing, I begged the universe that it wasn't Blaine with another woman. I hadn't seen his car in the parking lot. Swallowing my fear, I opened the door and gasped.

A woman with silver duct tape over her mouth banged her

feet. Looking closer, I saw that the same material constrained her ankles, and her hands were behind her back.

"Who are you?" I don't know why I asked that. The woman clearly couldn't speak.

The woman cried as she bobbed her head down toward her... very pregnant belly.

Who was this woman and why was she on our boat?

I said, "I'm going to take the tape off your mouth, okay?"

The woman nodded.

As I pulled the tape, I said, "I'm sorry," knowing it had to hurt.

Mouth freed, the woman said, "Help. We need help. Do you have a phone?"

Without a word, I hurried over to my purse and pulled out my phone to dial 9 1 1 when I heard footsteps and muffled voices from overhead. Before I could dial, footsteps turned into running, and two giant men in all black said, "Put it down."

I was frozen in fear.

The taller of the two men raised a gun and pointed it at me. "Who are you?" he asked.

With a shaking voice, I said, "I'm Sadie Jarreau. Who are you? This is my boat."

The two men exchanged glances.

The man with the gun said, "Give me the phone. Now."

I handed it to him, and he stuck it into his pocket.

The man without the gun said, "Stay there. Don't make a move. And be quiet."

The man without the gun hurried up top. It sounded like he made a phone call.

The pregnant woman's eyes darted all around, but the tears were still streaming. Too scared to speak, I tried to understand what was going on. Had those people kidnapped this woman and planned to use our boat as the getaway vehicle? How could this be happening in broad daylight in Alameda?

The other man came back and whispered into the man with the gun's ear. He directed his gaze to me. "In the bedroom, with the girl."

"What's happening here?"

He said, "Get in the bedroom, or I'll kill you."

Stunned, I stood frozen in place.

He growled, "Move!"

I knocked myself out of the trance and hurried to the bedroom where the tied-up woman sat. What would happen to us? The man with the gun shut the door to the bedroom and locked it from the outside. The woman continued to cry as we sat in the dark. I thought this day would change everything, and it did. It really did.

2

MARTINA

Under the fluorescent lights, my dress glittered like diamonds. It was a fitted gown with a strapless neckline and featured a rhinestone belt. It was elegant, and I actually kind of liked it. Who knew that at this point in my life, I wouldn't mind wearing a dress? I couldn't wait to show Zoey. She was going to be over the moon that I would wear such a feminine and sparkly piece of clothing. But then again, she was the one who had talked me into it. Well, her and Kim. When I'd accepted the role of groomsperson in Hirsch's upcoming wedding, he told me I could wear whatever I wanted. He said I could wear a suit like the groomsmen or I could wear a dress. That was one of the great things about my partner, Detective August Hirsch. He never tried to change me. Instead, he encouraged me to be myself and to focus on my strengths.

Kim clasped her hands together. "Do you love it?"

Smoothing down the sides of the dress, I said, "I honestly wasn't sure how I'd feel about being in a dress, but I like it. I don't think I've worn a dress since my wedding." It was true. Considering it was far from my typical attire, my flowing off-white gown had wowed Jared.

Gail, one of Kim's bridesmaids, said, "Martina, I didn't know you were married."

It had been three and a half years since Jared died, but each time someone inquired about him, it was like a jab to the heart. Time had certainly helped me cope and find a new normal, but the pain remained. It wasn't as sharp, but it was still there. "I was. My husband died a few years ago."

Gail said, "I'm so sorry."

"Thank you."

Gail, who was on her second glass of champagne, said, "Oh my gosh, Kim. I know exactly who we should set her up with."

Kim put her hand over her mouth and then removed it. "Yes!"

I did not like the direction this conversation was going. It was one thing to be clothed in sparkles, but it was quite another to be set up. I was a single mother with a ten-year-old daughter who worked as an investigator to catch murderers and find the missing with Hirsch by my side. I didn't date and wasn't sure if I would date again. "I should change back into my street clothes."

Kim's face fell. "Okay. You look great, by the way. You're a knockout, Martina."

"Thanks, Kim." I shuffled back into the dressing room and redressed in my uniform of black slacks and a black sweater with sensible shoes. My mind stuck on Kim and Gail's conversation about setting me up on a date. My life really hadn't turned out as I had expected. But I liked it. Maybe the idea of dating wasn't so terrible. I mean, I had taken on things that I never thought I would, and they turned out okay. I wore a dress, and I didn't hate it. I had a partner who was a cop, and I didn't hate it. In fact, Hirsch had become my best friend, and Kim was becoming a close second. But was I ready for such a big step?

Back in the lounge area, the bridesmaids and the bride-to-be, Kim, were sipping champagne. Gail handed me a flute.

"Oh, I don't drink," I said, as I rejected the glass for a second time. Kim gave her friend a look, like *I told you she's an alcoholic*. Kim knew I was a recovering alcoholic and had been for the last three years. Every day, it was a struggle, but that struggle seemed to lessen with time. I felt strong again, like my old self. Maybe even a little better. Older and wiser.

The woman who worked at the bridal salon must've heard the conversation because she rushed over with a flute of bubbly. She whispered, "It's apple cider."

I turned and gave her a smile. "Thank you." Not that I liked to drink sugar water either, but it was a special occasion.

Gail, the maid of honor, raised her glass. "Before we head out to lunch, I want to make a toast."

The bridal party raised their glasses. Gail continued, "To my girl, Kim. I love you and am so happy you found your other half. August is a lucky man. I wish you both a lifetime of love and happiness. Cheers."

Kim's blue eyes sparkled and mine welled up. *Dang it.* That got me. I said, "Cheers," with the others before sipping the overly sweet apple juice and heading out for lunch.

I rarely took long lunch breaks, but Kim was having a heck of a time trying to gather all of her bridesmaids and me, the groomsperson, at one time to do the initial fittings of the dresses. Technically, I was on the groom's side, but I wasn't wearing a black tux, so they grouped me with the chipper bridesmaid group who would be clad in bright fuchsia on the big day. Thankfully, I would be in black like the tuxes. I had agreed to a dress, but if they had forced me into fuchsia, it would have been a test of my friendship with Hirsch. Zoey, on the other hand, was delighted to be wearing a bright pink flower girl dress. She was in school and couldn't come for her dress fitting with the others, but Kim had promised her a special trip with just the three of us.

Seated at a local cantina, the bridesmaids' lunch was loud and energetic. Kim had bubbly, sweet friends — a lot like her. Half of them were schoolteachers, like Kim, and a few were in marketing. The women were friendly, albeit a bit young, not necessarily chronologically younger than me but younger.

After ordering a plate of fajitas, Gail cozied up next to Kim and me. "Okay, so we were talking. Kim told me you haven't been on a date since your husband died, which is totally cool, but if you want to dip your toe back into the dating pool, we know a guy."

I shook my head instinctively to stop whatever this was.

Kim said, "I promise he's a really nice guy. We all went to college with him. He's sweet and funny and recently divorced. He may not be Mr. Forever, but maybe he is a Mr. Try It Out Again, you know?"

"What's his name?" I asked, and almost instantly regretted the question.

"His name is Dave, and he's super nice and easy on the eyes, too."

Gail nodded. "Trust me, if I wasn't married, I'd be all over that."

Kim said, "And he's ex-military, so you have that in common."

"What branch?" I asked. Why was I encouraging this?

"Navy."

I said, "I suppose I could forgive that." What was I doing? This wedding was turning me into some kind of optimistic dreamer who believed I may have a second chance at love.

Kim and Gail erupted into laughter, and I joined them.

Being out with Kim and her friends, everything felt so normal, like the world was bright and shiny. Like my life was normal. Like I was a normal thirty-something, not somebody who hunted down bad guys and got shot every once in a while. Knock-on-wood that didn't happen again.

Kim said, "Okay, I'll set it up."

Shaking my head, I wondered what I'd just agreed to. "I'll need to check in with Zoey first. I need her to be okay with me dating again." Was I dating again? My phone buzzed, and I pulled it out from my bag. "What's up, Hirsch?"

"How's lunch?"

"It's fun. I think I got trapped into a date with somebody named Dave."

Hirsch laughed.

"What's up?" I asked again.

"Get your food to go. The paperwork is done, and we have an arrest warrant for our suspect in the death of Vanessa Carrington."

"Where did you find him?"

"A tip from a CI says he's been hiding out at his grandmother's house in downtown Oakland."

I glanced at my watch. "I could be at the station in thirty minutes."

"See you when you get here."

Kim wore a knowing look.

"I'm so sorry. That was Hirsch. We have a location on our suspect."

Kim held disappointment in her eyes but said, "No worries. I'm getting used to it with August. I'm sure they can wrap up your fajitas for you."

"Thanks, Kim, I'll see you later." I said goodbye to the women, who continued to chatter away and eat chips and guacamole.

I had a hard time believing this was my life now. Bridesmaids, dresses, dates, and partners. Life rarely turned out the way you thought it was going to, and mine was no exception.

VINCENT APPROACHED AND SLAPPED HIRSCH ON THE BACK. "Nice job, team."

I said, "Hopefully, that guy will spend the rest of his life behind bars and maybe a few more for good measure."

"No kidding. It won't bring Vanessa Carrington back to her parents, but at least they'll know that her killer is not free, and he can't hurt any other little girls."

The suspect was one of the worst kinds of people. If you could even call them people. A monster who kidnapped and murdered a four-year-old girl. He was suspected of a few others, but the forensics couldn't tie him to them. At least we had him behind bars, hopefully for the rest of his life. Sometimes, I thought that was too good for people like him. I'd learned in AA and my church that I was supposed to forgive. But how could you forgive that? There are people who need your forgiveness and people who need to be locked away and kept from everybody else so they don't inflict their horror on others.

We'd been lucky to find the suspect. If it wasn't for Hirsch's old CI from back when he was a homicide detective, we might not have caught him. Sometimes, that's what it took to solve a case — getting somebody to talk. All the forensics in the world couldn't always solve a case. Teamwork and witnesses talking to the police were usually the best recipe to catch the bad guys.

Vincent said, "I heard you were trying on fancy dresses."

"It had sparkles and everything."

Vincent clutched his chest and pretended to fall backward, as if having a cardiac event.

"Hilarious."

He laughed, and so did Hirsch. It didn't bother me. It had been a great day. I'd spent time with Kim and her friends, feeling like a carefree woman, and we'd caught the bad guy. Not too shabby.

Vincent said, "I'm only kidding. I can't wait to see everybody all dolled up at Hirsch's wedding."

"Me too."

"Kim is making it the affair to remember," Hirsch said with a giant smile on his face.

He was so in love. It was sweet.

Vincent said, "Well, since you're both in a good mood and you just solved a case, I have a request."

"What is it?" Hirsch asked.

Vincent was one of our top researchers and had recently started doing fieldwork too. He had never asked us for anything.

Vincent's typical jovial demeanor turned serious. "I don't know if it's against the rules or not, but there's a case I want to reopen. And I want the squad to work on it."

"Are we allowed to work on cases that have a personal connection?" I asked.

When I was working solely for my firm, Drakos Security and Investigations, we could work on whatever case we wanted. But since I had begun working with the CoCo County Sheriff's Department, I'd learned there were rules we had to follow. I didn't always like it, but I knew to keep my job, a job I loved, I had to follow them.

Hirsch said, "It depends. Does it involve a relative or someone you had a romantic relationship with?"

Vincent shook his head. "No, but it's important to me because it's important to Amanda. Will you consider it?"

"What kind of case?" I asked.

Vincent said, "Missing person."

Hirsch said, "Present us the case at tomorrow's briefing, and we'll see if we can take it on."

I gave Hirsch a bit of side-eye, knowing there was probably

no way we would turn down the case. But having Vincent present it to the entire squad was a good idea. We had solved a few major cases over the past few months, but I wasn't sure we were rested enough to take on another biggie.

Who was I kidding?

Hirsch and I never backed down from a challenge.

3

HIRSCH

Seated next to Martina, I waited for the rest of the Cold Case Squad room to fill up to start the morning briefing. I was curious to learn about the case Vincent wanted us to open for him. Would it be a straightforward one that the original investigators dropped the ball on, or would it be another doozy like our last few cases? Either way, I was sure Martina would want to take it on as much as I did. Unless, of course, there was something that would prohibit us from opening the case, like it was still active or there was a connection to one of us. I was doubtful, but you never know.

As the Cold Case Squad Leader, I couldn't say yes willy-nilly to every request the squad made. Not that the squad had made many requests. Actually, they had asked for very little from me, and I wanted to do whatever we could for Vincent.

"Kim told me she had a good time with you and the other girls at her bridesmaids' outing yesterday."

"It was fun. They're definitely a different crowd than I'm used to. I almost felt like a typical thirty-something woman."

I cracked a smile. "Kim really likes you. I'm glad you will be part of our wedding."

"Me too. I really don't think you could have found a better life partner, Hirsch."

"Save it for the speech," I said, trying not to get emotional right before our morning meeting.

Truth was, I was happier than I had ever been in my entire life. My job was challenging and brought me purpose. I had found a balance between the darkness of my job and the rest of the world with Kim. We would be married in just a few months, and I couldn't wait.

Kim was my sunshine. As sappy as that sounded, it was true. My thinking hadn't always been so optimistic, but I was a changed man who looked forward to Kim and my future together, including our upcoming wedding, where we would celebrate with our relatives and chosen family. I was definitely grateful for my life. I had always tried to remember that there was a lot to be thankful for. Life didn't always go as I hoped. And although I'd been in law enforcement for twenty years, my brother's case was still cold. He was the reason I went into the Academy and why I wanted to be on this side of the fence. When I entered the police force, my goal was to make sure other families didn't have to go through what mine had. They never caught my brother's killer, and it was difficult to accept.

With the team in place, I said, "Morning, squad."

The team replied with hoots and hollers and good mornings. They were an energetic crew. "We'll get updates, and then we'll have a presentation from our very own Vincent, who is going to propose we re-open a special cold case of his choosing."

"Why don't we have Vincent go first? There's no new information on our case. How about you guys?" Ross asked.

Wolf said, "Same here."

Jayda nodded. "Same here. We're still waiting for DNA from the lab. We pounded the pavement and canvassed around the original crime scene, but until DNA comes back, we're playing the waiting game."

I looked at Vincent.

He nodded.

Vincent was known for being a silly guy, always laughing and teasing. This was one of the few times he was as serious as he was right now. He flicked on the projector and began.

On the first slide was a woman with bright blue eyes and shoulder-length blonde hair. I had to do a double take. She looked a lot like Kim.

Vincent said, "This is Sadie Jarreau. At the time of her disappearance, she was a thirty-five-year-old nurse from Moraga and married to Dr. Blaine Jarreau. She went missing five years ago. Last known location Alameda marina. They found her car parked in the marina parking lot, but she was nowhere to be found."

"Did they have surveillance cameras at the marina?" I asked.

"Yes, but there was a malfunction that day, and they had erased the video before they even knew Sadie was missing."

"Was the husband cleared, or was he the prime suspect?" Ross asked.

"He wasn't officially cleared, but they couldn't find a motive, and he had an alibi."

"When did he report her missing?" Martina asked.

"He didn't. Sadie was reported missing by her best friend and coworker, May Donovan. May reported Sadie missing when she didn't show up for her shift at the hospital the next day. Full disclosure — May Donovan is my girlfriend, Amanda's, sister. That's how I know about the case."

The personal connection was there, but it was pretty loose. "Did you ever meet Sadie?" I asked.

"No."

No problem there. "In that case, there is no issue reopening the file. What were the original theories?"

"The original investigators had two theories. One is that she died by suicide and chose a watery grave near her husband's beloved boat. Apparently, the marriage was a little rocky, and she'd been depressed, according to her husband and even May. Second is that the husband did something to her, but there's no evidence pointing to him."

"What was Sadie doing at the marina that day?" Martina asked.

"According to May, she'd left work early to surprise her husband on the boat. She was going to prepare a dinner for them, trying to rekindle their relationship."

A husband caught by surprise?

"Sounds pretty suspicious to me. He doesn't report his wife missing. The marriage is on the rocks, and he's got a boat."

Wolf shrugged. "My money's on the husband."

I looked at Vincent, who remained dead serious. "What else can you tell us? What else do you know about the husband?" I asked.

"Local doctor, a general practitioner, and a clinician working a few nights a week at the hospital."

Wolf said, "A doctor would know how to dispose of a body."

Jayda shrugged.

I said, "What was his alibi for the day she went missing?"

"He said he was at work and got home late — after midnight. Went to bed, she wasn't there, but he said sometimes she fell asleep in the den watching TV, so he thought nothing of it."

"Did they check phone records to see if he called to see where she was?"

"It's not in the file."

"You look through the file, Vincent?" Martina asked.

"I did."

"On a scale from one to ten, how well did they investigate it?"

"Between these walls only, I'd give them a four. When there weren't any leads, they just gave up."

Martina nudged me lightly. "We can find her."

I had to love her confidence. "Where did Sadie work?"

"Bay General. She's a pediatric nurse."

"Is May also a nurse?"

"Yes."

"Does she still work at the hospital?"

"Yes."

"Do we know the origin of the marital problems? Was there infidelity?"

"No reported infidelity — from Blaine — according to the statements, but May said Sadie suspected Blaine was having an affair."

"Why?"

Vincent said, "Don't know. May might be able to tell you more."

"Was suicide ruled out?" Martina asked.

"No. But she couldn't have taken the boat out, offed herself, and then drove the boat back to their slip."

"The boat was still at the slip when she was reported missing?" I asked.

"Yes."

"Any chance she had help?"

"Nothing obvious, but they never found her body."

"Anyone check with the Coast Guard to see if the boat had been sighted out that day?" Martina asked.

"They did. The Coast Guard said there weren't any reports about the boat, but it didn't mean she hadn't taken it out."

Martina nodded. "I think we'll find out in time if the

husband is involved or if she really ended her own life. Any chance she ran off to start a new life?"

"May didn't think so. And they talked every single day at work."

Vincent stared at me. "Well done. Martina and I will take the case since we just closed ours. We'll start working on it today. Questions, Martina?"

"I may have more questions once we look through the case files and the evidence. I'm assuming May is more than happy to talk to us now, Vincent?"

"Yes. She brought it up over Christmas, and I told her I wasn't sure if we could bring up cases for discussion. She said she really wants to know what happened to Sadie."

"What does May think happened to her?"

"That Blaine killed her. She said there was something about him that creeped her out, and she didn't trust him."

Nodding, I thought this could be an interesting case.

I agreed with Martina. We would find Sadie Jarreau, and whoever took her would be brought to justice.

4

SADIE

Sitting on the bench across from the bed where the pregnant woman sat, I couldn't believe any of this was happening. Who were those men and who were they taking orders from? The pregnant woman continued to whimper. In a low voice, in an attempt to calm her, I said, "I'm Sadie. What's your name?"

"Rosa."

I tried to smile to let her know I was on her side. I wasn't sure what Rosa was doing there or how she got there or who those men were, but I was fairly certain I was Team Rosa, not Team Thug. Staring at Rosa and her belly, I figured she had to be at least eight months pregnant.

"When are you due?"

"In a few weeks."

"Do you know if you're having a boy or a girl?"

"A girl," she said with tears in her eyes.

Why had they taken her? "How long have you been here on this boat?"

"They brought me here earlier today."

"Where are you from?"

"Bakersfield."

"How did you get here? Do you know those men?"

She shook her head. "No. I was walking to the grocery store when a van pulled up, and someone grabbed me and put me in the back. The next thing I knew, I was here."

If she was from Bakersfield, there wouldn't be anything about her disappearance on the local news. That was probably why I hadn't seen her face on television. Nobody would know she was on my husband's 46-foot yacht in Alameda. My brain screamed that we needed a way off this boat and away from those men as fast as humanly possible.

"Did they take you too?" Rosa asked.

"No. This is my boat. I came here to prepare a dinner for my husband. I don't know who those people are or how they could get you on board."

This was all so perplexing.

Blaine had purchased the boat two years before. He'd explained it had always been a dream of his and that the extravagant purchase was a good investment. I had wanted to make him happy, so I didn't question it, but I never imagined when he held up those keys with the floating device attached that this was how it would end.

Footsteps sounded.

The door to the stateroom flung open, and the man with the gun reappeared. "We just got orders. We're going on a little trip. The both of you will be quiet, or there will be consequences. Do you understand?"

Rosa said, "Yes."

I nodded and tried to think of the last time we had been on the boat — at least a few weeks. It could easily have been broken into and used by these awful people after that. The man handed us a bag. "This will keep you for a while. I'm guessing you know where the head is?" he asked me.

"Yes."

"Good." He then approached Rosa and pulled a knife from his hip.

Rosa's eyes widened.

"I'm just taking off the tape. Turn around."

She complied.

That was a good sign, right?

When Rosa was free, the man said to me, "You take care of her, and we'll all be okay. No funny business," before exiting, shutting the door behind him.

I picked up the grocery bag and looked inside. Water bottles, sandwiches, chips, cookies, and bananas. They must've just gone out to purchase these. There was a market not too far from the marina.

We needed to think of a way to get off this boat. It was the middle of the day, and I knew there weren't many recreational weekend boaters out, but one of those living on their boats had to have seen something, and I knew there were security cameras positioned around the marina. How had nobody seen the armed men and their hostage? I heard the roar of the engine, and my heart sank. We were going somewhere. Where? What would happen to us?

The man's tone toward me had changed. Friendly, almost. I had never seen either man before and wasn't sure how they could be people who kidnapped pregnant women and let me go. It didn't jive. If they let me go, what would happen to Rosa and her baby girl?

I took the items out of the bag and handed a bottle of water to Rosa. She needed to stay hydrated.

"Thanks."

After she took a hearty gulp, I passed her the other food items. I had zero appetite but knew I would need my strength if I were to come up with a plan.

The boat rocking increased, and I clutched the wall. I glanced up at Rosa, who was having a hard time staying upright. "If it's more comfortable, you can sit down here with me."

She climbed off the bed and joined me on the bench. "How are you feeling?"

"Other than terrified?"

I nodded. "I'm a nurse. Do you mind if I check your pulse?"

She reached out her wrist. I pressed my fingers to her pulse. It was faster than it should be, but that wasn't surprising, considering someone had kidnapped her. "Is the baby kicking? Moving around?"

"Yes, she's the only reason I haven't completely fallen apart."

"I'm so sorry. Have they said why they took you? Or anything to explain any of this?"

She shook her head. "No, it all happened so fast."

The engine let up, and the boat bobbed. Were they taking us to the middle of the ocean to dump our bodies?

Instinctively, I lifted a finger to my lips so we could hear what was happening. The men yelled toward someone. Someone yelled back.

I hurried over to the portal and saw that we were side by side with a much larger boat. Maybe a 100-foot yacht — it was huge. I doubted this was good news.

The door opened, and I stood up, as did Rosa. The man with the gun said, "Come with me. We're moving to another boat. Please don't be afraid."

Not be afraid? I nodded and took Rosa's hand and led her off the bench and up the stairs to the dock. There were three other men and one female with reddish-brown hair on the yacht.

The crew of the yacht helped us aboard and ushered us onto the massive vessel. A man and the woman led us below deck, past a huge galley and down a hallway. The new man with a gun on his hip said, "Stay here."

I watched as the woman led Rosa into the room and closed the door behind her. What were they going to do with her? I wished I would have asked Rosa her last name on the off chance I got out of this alive. Would I ever see her again?

At least when we were on my boat, we were together, and it felt a bit less lonely. Less hopeless. They led me down the hall, opened another door into another stateroom. Probably the master based on its massive size. What on Earth was going on? And, more importantly, what were they going to do with us?

5

MARTINA

LEANING OVER SADIE JARREAU'S CASE FILE, I COULDN'T believe what I was reading. The original investigators had sworn there was no motive or obvious evidence the husband had done something to his wife. However, when they searched the boat, the crime scene investigators hadn't found a single fingerprint, footprint, or trace of anyone ever stepping foot on it. But the CSI team had noted it smelled of bleach. That hadn't caught anybody's attention?

The more I read, the more I was convinced a crime had occurred on the vessel and had been covered up with bleach. A doctor would know that bleach would erase DNA. Why had they let Blaine Jarreau off the hook? If I'd been the original investigator, I'd be chasing him around town until I got him to confess.

My body was tense. I told myself to calm down and that I needed to not jump to conclusions.

Hirsch said, "What is it?"

"Tell me what you think of this." I slid the file over to him.

He read it and shook his head. "Not a single print and smelling of bleach?"

"Yeah, and look at the statement from the husband. The investigator didn't even ask him about it."

"That's absurd. Who uses bleach to clean a boat? Somebody trying to cover up a heinous crime, that's who."

"I agree."

"Let's pay the good doctor a visit."

"I'm ready."

With that, Hirsch swiped his keys off the table, and we left the sheriff's station to talk to Dr. Blaine Jarreau about his missing wife.

WE ARRIVED IN THE STRIP MALL TYPE MEDICAL CENTER that housed Dr. Blaine Jarreau's family practice. Hirsch and I both felt it was important we didn't call ahead. He didn't need to know we were coming so that he could hide whatever evidence he may be holding on to. We also didn't want him to prepare his answers. We wanted an honest, unrehearsed reaction to better gauge if he was our guy.

Parked and armed with a game plan, we strolled up to the receptionist. Hirsch said, "We're here to see Dr. Jarreau."

"Do you have an appointment?"

Hirsch said, "No, but we need to speak with him. It's about his wife."

The receptionist's hazel eyes popped wide open. "Did you find her?"

Edging my way in, I said, "Not yet. Did you know Sadie?"

"Of course. I've worked for Dr. Jarreau for several years. Sadie is such a lovely woman. I hope you find her."

"And what is your name?"

"Vicki Lowden."

"How long have you worked here?"

"Ten years. I've been with Dr. Jarreau since the very beginning."

"What was his relationship like with his wife?"

She lowered her voice. "They were okay. When they first married, they were deeply in love, but then the strain of not being able to conceive really took a toll on both of them."

"You must've been close with the doctor and Sadie."

"Sadie and I would go to lunch sometimes. And during the holidays, they would host a party at their house for all the staff and their family and friends. Sadie and Dr. Jarreau were a beautiful couple. It broke my heart they couldn't have children."

Could the infertility be a motive for suicide? "How has Dr. Jarreau been since his wife went missing?"

"When it first happened, he was devastated. He even closed the practice for a few weeks and had me reschedule all of his appointments. He was beside himself."

That could mean any number of things. He could have been remorseful he had killed his wife in a fit of rage or during an argument. It wouldn't be the first time a killer didn't have a history of violence. "Anything else you can tell us about Sadie and Dr. Jarreau?"

"No, but I sure hope you find her."

"Thank you, Miss Lowden. Can you let the doctor know we need to speak to him?"

"Of course." She scurried back into the offices.

We stepped away from the window, and not two minutes later, the door from the lobby into the medical office popped open. A man balding at the temples with bloodshot eyes and a white coat said, "Detectives, please come back with me."

We followed him past exam rooms and rounded the corner into an office. "Please have a seat."

Seated, Hirsch said, "I'm Detective Hirsch with the CoCo

County Cold Case Squad, and this is my partner, Martina Monroe."

Hirsch handed over his business card, and I did the same.

"This is about Sadie?" he asked.

Beads of sweat were forming on his temple.

I said, "It is. We have reopened your wife's missing persons case."

"That's great. How can I help?" he asked with the hint of apprehension.

Guilty? "We need you to tell us when you realized your wife was missing."

He nodded. "I hadn't realized she was missing until the police showed up at my door. Kind of like right now. I got home from work. It was a clinic night, so it was around 1 AM. I went straight to bed. Sadie wasn't there, but I didn't think much of it. She often fell asleep in front of the TV. I went to sleep and got up the next morning and went to work. I didn't see her that day and assumed she had an early shift at the hospital."

"Was that normal that you didn't see her at night or in the morning, either?" I asked.

"Sometimes our shifts would conflict. More and more, it seemed like we were two ships in the night."

Interesting phrasing. "How was your marriage?"

"It was hard. Everything started great. We were happy, and I thought I was the luckiest man alive to have Sadie as my partner. After we got married, we couldn't wait to start a family. Shortly after the wedding, we tried to conceive, but nine months later, I grew concerned, and we met with a fertility specialist and began a round of testing to determine why it wasn't happening. Long story short, four years later and multiple rounds of IVF, we still weren't pregnant. It was hard. It was especially hard on Sadie. Every time she took a pregnancy test and it came back negative, she cried. Every time she got her period, she cried. I wished there was something I could do to give her a baby, but I failed her," he said, sadly.

Had I read him wrong? It didn't feel like the kind of grief from an accident. The vibe was more that he cared about his wife and was sad he couldn't make her happy. But then again, maybe he offed Sadie to move on to the next wife, one who could have a baby. "Did you find the source of your fertility issues?"

He shook his head. "No. The endocrinologist said that it was unexplained infertility. Neither one of us had anything medically wrong with us. Once we found that out, we tried everything to have a more relaxing, stress-free environment to help with conception, but the efforts were in vain."

"Was there any infidelity in the marriage?" Hirsch asked.

He shook his head. "No, never, not even now. She's been gone five years, and I haven't been on a single date. I loved Sadie since the day I met her."

Hirsch and I exchanged puzzled looks. I understood the confusion. On one hand, Blaine Jarreau appeared to be a grieving husband but was also extremely worried that we were reopening the case. The two sentiments rarely went together.

"And Sadie never stepped out?" Hirsch asked.

"Not that I know of."

"When was the last time you saw your wife?"

Dr. Blaine Jarreau glanced down and scratched the back of his head. "It was the day before May reported her missing. She was getting ready for work, and I was just getting up."

"Did you have a conversation?"

"Just the usual good morning, and how did you sleep?"

"How did she seem? Was she happier or more sad than usual?"

"She'd been depressed for so long about not having a family, but that morning, she was more chipper than usual. The therapist said her mood could change once she had come to terms with the fact that we couldn't conceive."

"Did you inquire about her good mood?"

"No. I wish I had."

"Do you know where your wife is right now?" Hirsch asked.

He stared directly at Detective Hirsch and paused. "No."

"Is there something you're not telling us, Dr. Jarreau?" I asked.

"No, of course not. I'm just surprised that you're asking about Sadie. I didn't know you were coming down. If I had known, I could've rearranged my appointments, or I could have come down to see you at the station."

"Do you think it's possible Sadie took her own life?" I asked.

"There were some pretty dark days. But no, I don't think so. Despite the continued disappointment, she never gave up hope. I don't think Sadie would ever give up hope."

That's interesting. If he had killed Sadie, I would have expected that he would push the suicide theory, deflecting blame from him.

"Did she have suicidal thoughts?"

"Never."

"Does Sadie have family in the area?"

"No. She grew up in the foster system. She never knew her biological parents. I think that's why it was so important for her to have a family. Sadie was tough. She had overcome so much to survive her childhood and go to college to become a nurse. She's the strongest woman I've ever known and not somebody who would harm herself."

"You're familiar with May Donovan?"

He nodded. "She's Sadie's best friend."

"Have you spoken with her since Sadie went missing?"

"No, not since right after we did our search." He looked at

me and then at Hirsch. "I know she thinks I did something to Sadie, but I didn't. I swear it."

"Reviewing the case files, we noticed that the crime scene investigators picked up the scent of bleach on your boat when they searched it. Is that something you typically would do — clean your boat with bleach?" I asked.

He nodded. "I did. I don't know if you have any experience with fishing, but the odor of rotten fish is pretty noxious. Sometimes the juices from the fish were hard to pick up, so a couple of months after getting the boat, I switched cleaning products over to bleach. The bleach kills the bacteria that causes the fish smell."

"So, you're not surprised that bleach was found on the boat right after your wife went missing?"

"No."

"Do you clean the boat yourself?"

"If I've been out fishing, I'd clean up right afterward using bleach wipes. But once a month, I had a cleaning crew conduct a routine clean."

I wasn't sure about his story. I wasn't familiar with fishing or cleaning up fish odors, but I had never heard of bleach as being the top choice for that. Although the bleach wipe was easy to use and would be convenient to wipe down everything as you exited. "Do you still use the same cleaning crew you did before?"

"I don't have the boat anymore."

"What happened to it?" I asked.

"I sold it a few months after Sadie disappeared."

Getting rid of evidence? "Why?"

"It cost quite a bit to maintain, and with Sadie gone, I only have my salary. It was get rid of the boat or the house."

He needed the money? Once Dr. Jarreau's financials were back, we'd be able to verify.

"Is there anything you could tell us that might help us find your wife? Maybe something that you didn't remember back then but have since had time to think about?" Hirsch asked.

"No."

"Seems pretty quiet in the office. Not many patients today?"

"I've cut back on new patients. I'm getting a little older, and working both the practice and at the hospital has taken a toll. At this point, I am at half capacity. I'm phasing out my clients so that I only need to come in Tuesday through Thursday."

Fewer patients could explain the reduction in cash flow and why he sold the boat. "Four-day weekend sounds nice."

Dr. Jarreau had nothing in response to that.

I said, "If you think of anything else that may be related to your wife's disappearance, please let us know."

"Of course."

"You have a nice day, Dr. Jarreau," Hirsch said as we exited.

Back in Hirsch's car, I said, "I wouldn't rule him out."

"Neither would I."

6

HIRSCH

Dr. Jarreau was a tough nut to crack. Half of the time while we interviewed him, I believed he was sad about his wife's disappearance, but the other half of the time, he was sending off a strong guilty signal. Although that didn't always mean guilt for the crime that was being investigated. He may have done nothing sinister to his wife, but he could be hiding something else. For whatever unknown reason, Blaine wasn't thrilled we were looking into Sadie's disappearance. Not typical of a grieving husband. If he truly had nothing to do with her disappearance, one would think he would be happy we hadn't given up hope of finding her alive. It would be interesting to learn what the team found in his background.

I wanted to know everything there was to know about Blaine Jarreau. Like where he grew up, where he went to school, past relationships, everything. No stone unturned. Nine times out of ten, if a person went missing, it was because of somebody they know — like their spouse.

But I couldn't ignore the fact that, according to the case files, the day Sadie went missing, Dr. Jarreau was in his office and had several members of the staff including the other doctor who worked in the building confirm he been working there all day and then was at the hospital that night working in the clinic. We would need to re-interview the staff at the hospital and his practice to confirm the original statements to ensure Dr. Jarreau's alibi was solid. If our last big case taught me anything, it was that you couldn't always count on the previous investigation for facts pertaining to the case or the suspects.

Martina and I had a pretty exemplary track record, and neither one of us wanted to ruin it. We were in this business to bring closure to families and help them with their grieving process or, better yet, reunite them with loved ones. And it was exactly what we intended to do.

Knocking me out of my thoughts, Martina said, "It's right there."

Nodding, I pulled up in front of May Donovan's home. She was Sadie's best friend and coworker at the hospital where she worked. She was also the person who had reported Sadie missing and our very own Vincent's girlfriend's sister.

We rarely took on personal cases, but it was far enough removed that it should be fine with no conflict of interest. Plus, it was one missing person. Relating to Sadie's disappearance, I didn't get serial killer vibes or a bigger, more systemic issue. If I could channel Martina's gut, I'd say it was the husband — whether he did the deed himself or had someone else do it — or suicide. Hopefully, this would be a relatively open and shut case. It would be nice to have an easy win for once. Maybe forensics would crack the case wide open.

We hurried up the front steps. Before I could raise my arm to knock, the door opened. A woman with bright green eyes and long, auburn hair smiled. "Detective Hirsch and Martina?"

"That's right."

She said, "I'm May. Please come in." She led us down the hallway into a sitting room with a fireplace and portraits of May and her sister, Amanda, whom I had met a few times. The two bore a striking resemblance. Other family photos hung on the walls of children with missing teeth and one that I assumed was the family dog. The home was bright and cheery. I looked forward to the day that Kim and I were hanging our wedding photos on the wall, along with a few family portraits that brightened our home as well.

May said, "Please have a seat."

We sat, and she said, "Thank you so much for reopening the case. When I asked Vincent about it, he told me he wasn't sure if it was against the rules or not, since, well, he's dating my sister."

"We discussed it, and we think that the relationship is distant enough that there's no conflict of interest."

"I'm so happy to hear that."

Martina said, "You have a lovely home, May. You and Amanda look so much alike. If I didn't already know, I would have guessed that you were sisters."

Martina was good with the icebreakers and making our interviewees comfortable.

"Yes, Amanda is a much younger version of me. She's my little sister, and I'd do anything for her. We like Vincent too."

"We're pretty fond of Vincent as well." Martina shrugged. "He kinda grows on you."

May chuckled. "That he does."

"So, what can you tell us about Sadie?" Martina transitioned beautifully.

"Well, she was one of the kindest, most intelligent, most optimistic people that I know."

"What did you think of Blaine?"

"Never liked him." She shook her head as if in disgust. "Something about him just rubbed me the wrong way. It was like he gave off this aura that he was better than other people. From what I understand, he comes from money. Sadie felt a little intimidated when she joined their family. They were from a pretty expensive area. The parents are very wealthy, and they all looked out for each other. Sadie, I don't know if you realize this, was basically an orphan since the time she was four years old. She grew up in the foster system. So, for her to join a family of bluebloods like the Jarreaus, well, she was like a fish out of water. I told her any insecurities she had were nonsense. She is one of the most intelligent, kind, and tough women I've ever known."

"Did their difference in backgrounds ever cause any issues in the marriage?" Martina asked.

"No, but I think when they could not produce an heir to the Jarreau family, there was tension. But to be fair, it was really hard on Sadie. The years of trying to conceive wore on her, but she's so optimistic and cheerful. She never gave up, but it was like every time she took a pregnancy test, it chewed away at her soul. She would make an exceptional mother."

"Had they considered adoption?"

"I think Sadie was open to it, considering her background, but Blaine was against it. At first, anyhow. She said that she thought he was warming up, but then things took a turn."

"How so?" I asked.

"He started keeping strange hours. Started having more nights at the hospital and taking late-night phone calls, that kind of thing. She thought he was cheating."

"Was he?" I asked.

"She never had evidence, but she suspected he was hiding things from her. Keeping secrets from your wife usually means cheating. She'd also said that he had become distant with her. She thought maybe her drive to continue with IVF was causing it, so she finally agreed to take a break from the fertility treatments. It was hard on both of them. But like I said, she wasn't one to give up and was hopeful for her marriage still. The day before I reported her missing, she left work early because she planned to make a special dinner for Blaine on the boat. It's really a yacht. I don't know if you've seen it — 47 feet."

"Was Blaine supposed to meet her there?"

"He didn't know that she would be there. But he told her after work he was going to his boat, so she planned to surprise him. When she left work that day, it was like there was a renewed spark inside of her, like the old Sadie before the years of infertility had gotten to her. She was definitely in a good mood when she left work."

Dr. Jarreau failed to mention he had planned to be at his boat that night — or had at least told Sadie that.

"Any idea why the good mood?" I asked.

May exhaled. "This is just speculation, and I could be completely off base, but I am a nurse. For a few months before she disappeared, she seemed a little more tired, and I wondered if..."

"If she was pregnant?" Martina asked.

"Yeah. It fits, right? She was tired, more tired than normal, and then was very excited and was going to surprise Blaine with dinner. I didn't tell her my suspicions, but I remember feeling joy for her if that was what was really going on. Of all people who deserve to have a happy ending in a happy family, it was Sadie." May's eyes welled.

"What do you think happened to her?" I asked, since I was always interested in a key witness's theories. Sometimes, they were right on. And sometimes, they were way off base, but often, the simplest explanation was the actual one.

May sniffled. "I wondered if Blaine was there that night on the boat. Maybe she surprised him, and he was there with another woman and got rid of her."

"You think Blaine killed her?"

May nodded. "I do. There's no other explanation."

Martina said, "You've been very helpful."

I added, "Yes, you have been. Is there anything else you can tell us about Sadie that might help us find out what happened to her?"

"Just that I hope you find her. Find out what happened to her. She didn't deserve what he did to her."

May was awfully confident that Blaine had killed his wife. Her scenario seemed plausible. If Blaine didn't know she would be on his boat that night but then showed up there when he was already preoccupied with a mistress, he could've lost his temper. If Blaine had been on the boat that night and brought a woman there, we could find that woman, and we might get a break in this case. "Any idea who Dr. Jarreau may have been seeing?"

May shook her head. "No, Sadie never found out the identity of the woman."

It sounded like we needed to pay Dr. Jarreau another visit and ask why he'd told Sadie he would be at the boat that night.

7

MARTINA

THE TIMEX ON MY WRIST TOLD ME WE ONLY HAD ABOUT AN hour of daylight remaining. There were so many questions unanswered about Sadie's disappearance, it compelled me to continue. "Hey, Hirsch, what do you say we swing by the marina real quick and see if anyone remembers seeing Sadie Jarreau the day she went missing?"

He cocked his head. "It's a weekday. We may not find too many people around."

"I'm sure we'll catch a few who are retired or living on their boats. They're the ones most likely to have seen something."

"That's a good point. Let's stop by the marina, and then we'll head back to the station. It's getting late."

Before Kim, Hirsch was never concerned with how late it was getting. If I didn't know any better, I'd say he was a changed man. That wasn't necessarily a bad thing.

"All-righty." If anyone could confirm they saw Sadie get on the boat but never off, we may have probable cause to search Blaine's boat and home. Of course, if we did, we'd also have to track down the boat, but it could help us determine its movements that night — assuming the onboard computer kept a log of where it traveled.

Despite growing up on an island, I wasn't ever into the boating scene. I lived in a trailer and not a house with water views and its own dock. Boats are a luxury item that are expensive to buy and maintain. I didn't grow up with that kind of money.

While Hirsch drove, I pulled the case files from my backpack and skimmed through the pages to see which slip had belonged to Blaine Jarreau. The slip number would tell us where to canvas the area for witnesses. It was a bit of a long shot since five years had passed, but if we could find a few boat owners who'd docked there for over five years, we would be in good shape.

For Sadie's case, we had to investigate all avenues. Even though Vincent never knew Sadie, in my book, Amanda was part of our team — our family. The two had been together for over a year, which made her one of us, whether she liked it or not. And her sister was an extension of that family. We had to find out what happened to Sadie.

Hirsch pulled up to the parking lot that overlooked the dark blue waters with dozens and dozens of docked boats. The parking lot was half-full, which made me think we had a pretty good chance of finding a witness or two. Or maybe I was just overly optimistic with the start of the new year and the fact I had become a person who wore sparkly gowns.

The skies were gray, and the water was choppy. It wasn't a great day for smooth sailing. It made me queasy just thinking about it. "The Jarreau boat was in slip 17. It's over there in that direction," I said, pointing to the left.

We approached a locked gate, based on the signage, only accessible by boat owners. Hirsch said, "We can either wait for somebody to let us in, or we can call the harbormaster."

As Hirsch finished his words, I spotted movement from the corner of my eye and waved. I nudged Hirsch. "Take out your badge."

Hirsch hesitated momentarily but then pulled out his badge and held it up in the air. The figure drew closer and hurried toward the gate. It was a man in his sixties wearing a tie-dyed, long-sleeve tee. "What can I do for you, officer?"

"We're investigating the disappearance of a woman last seen here five years ago. We're hoping to get inside and look around. Maybe ask a few questions of anyone who might be out."

The gentleman opened the gate. "No problem. Anything I can help with?"

As we walked toward the boats, I asked, "What's your name, sir?"

He stopped walking. "The name is Drake Porter."

Hirsch said, "I'm Detective Hirsch, and this is my partner, Martina."

"Nice to meet you. Is there anything I can help with?"

"How long have you kept your boat here?"

"Well, geez, I'd say just about fifteen years now."

Jackpot. "Which slip is yours?" I asked.

"I'll show you. I'm in slip 15."

Perfect. We approached his shiny boat, and I wondered if he waxed it regularly. It appeared to be in pristine condition. "How often are you out here on your boat?" I asked.

"Every day since I retired. The wife prefers I'm out of her hair during the day. I usually go home at night for dinner if she's made something good." He chortled.

"How long ago did you retire?"

"Ten years this June."

"How's retirement treating you?"

"It's pretty great."

"That's good to hear. Say, do you remember the boat that

used to be docked in slip 17?"

"The Jarreau boat?"

"That's the one."

"I figured that maybe the missing person case you were looking into. They still haven't found her?"

"No. Were you here the day she went missing?"

"I wasn't. But I heard about it the next day. My buddy in slip 16 could probably help you out. He was there the day she disappeared and the next morning, too."

"Really?"

"If anybody saw anything, it was him."

I didn't recall seeing any witnesses' statements from any of the neighboring boats. All the investigation report had said about the marina was that there were no working security cameras and that no one had seen Sadie that day.

They'd believed she was there was because of May's statement and the fact that her car was in the parking lot. Anyone could assume she actually went on the boat, but nobody had corroborated that she had, in fact, gone down to the dock and was waiting on her husband's boat.

"You've been mighty helpful, Drake."

"Sure thing. Go have a knock on my neighbor's door. His name is Sam — a nice guy as long as you don't cross him."

"Thanks." Drake waved and headed back over to his boat. My adrenaline was pumping, and I could feel we were getting close to finding more answers instead of more questions.

Hirsch tapped on the side of the boat. He said, "Fingers crossed."

"Fingers crossed." Maybe this would be a short case — that would be great. We'd had a couple of real challenging cases last year, and I could use a break in all the excitement. Not to mention, it sure would be nice to find Sadie sooner rather than later.

A few moments later, a man with unkempt, long, gray hair and a scruffy beard emerged. "What do you want?"

"My name's Detective Hirsch. This is my partner, Martina. Can we speak with you for a few moments?"

"What's this about?"

Friendly. "We're investigating the disappearance of Sadie Jarreau five years ago. Her husband's boat was docked next door."

The man's demeanor changed, and his face softened. He climbed out and stood out on the dock. "I'm Sam Sutton and I remember Sadie."

"You do?"

"I do. I remember that day too."

"What do you remember?"

"Well, I saw Sadie climb on the boat with a grocery bag in her arms. I'd only seen her a couple of times before that day. I was out most of the day because I prefer being out in the open water rather than on the dock. I'm usually out on the sea, and it was a nice day. That day, I was just coming back, and when I saw her walking toward the boat, I waved as I docked."

"Did you see her leave the marina?"

"I didn't. But I didn't stop and talk to her or anything like that. I was out on the water all day, so I had gone down to the head to get cleaned up. When I came up on deck, the Jarreau boat was gone."

"Did you see anybody else on the boat?"

"No, and I didn't hear anything or see anything either, but that doesn't mean somebody hadn't gotten on when I was downstairs cleaning up with my music on. Like I said, when I came up to have my dinner, the boat was gone. Normally, I wouldn't take much notice, but when she went missing the next day, it stuck in my memory."

"Did you ever see anybody else on the boat with Blaine or

Sadie?"

"No, but I'm usually out during the day, and I like to do overnights on Catalina or down the coast as often as I can. I live on my boat and try not to stay docked for too long. I saw Blaine a few times. He seemed nice enough."

"But no other women?"

"No, never."

If Sadie got on the boat that day, had she been alone? Had Blaine shown up and murdered her and then dumped her body out at sea? "When was the next time you saw the boat back in the slip?"

"When I got up the next morning, the boat was there."

"Did you hear it return?"

Sam shook his head. "No, but I sleep like the dead. Which is why I'm able to live out here. Nothing disturbs my sleep."

"Anything else you could tell us about the Jarreaus or anybody else you may have seen hanging around that day?"

"Nope, that's it. She was there. She took the boat out, or someone took the boat out, and docked it the next morning. Nothing suspicious about it."

"Thank you very much."

"Any time."

Hirsch and I questioned a few more folks on the docks who had no information relating to our case, other than it was normal for the cameras to malfunction from time to time and that their system was due for an upgrade.

After we hurried back to the car, I said, "Someone had to have been with Sadie that day. I don't think she would have taken the boat out on her own if she was planning a special dinner."

Hirsch said, "Agreed. Now we need to find out who that person was."

My thoughts exactly.

8

SADIE

It had been two days since they took us to the large yacht, several hours off the coast of Alameda. I did not know where we were, but I supposed it was a good sign that they fed us, or at least I thought they did. One man would bring in meals three times a day to me, and I assumed they did the same for Rosa. The situation was terrifying, but I couldn't imagine what Rosa must be going through. Eight months pregnant, thrown into a van, put on a boat, and sent off to sea. My situation wasn't much better, but I still had hope we could get out of this alive.

Nobody had come to talk to me or explain the situation. They had inflicted no physical pain on me, just the threat of it. If I tried to leave or didn't do as they said, would they make good on their promise of violence?

Somebody had to be looking for us. Was Blaine frantically calling the police and organizing search parties? What about Rosa's family? Work would surely notice I hadn't shown up for my shift. They must be worried about me. May and I usually spoke several times a day. If no one else, she would come looking for me. I was sure they were all looking, but would they ever find me?

Footsteps stomped down the stairs toward the staterooms. I wasn't sure how many people were on the boat with us. But based on the sounds I'd heard, there was at least one person who checked on Rosa and myself and a few others for a total of four. Faint sounds of voices echoed down the hall, and I tiptoed over to the door. With my ear pressed up against it, the muffled sounds were hard to decipher, but I thought they said something about carrying Rosa out of her room. Where would they transport her to? Why couldn't she walk on her own?

Someone knocked on Rosa's door in rapid succession before they opened it. The courtesy was odd, considering she was being held captive. Rosa screamed, "No! No! No!" over and over.

My body shook.

What were they doing to her?

A woman's voice said, "You must come with us. We have to keep the baby safe."

Concerned with the baby's safety? That must be a positive sign. Where were they taking Rosa and her unborn baby? Did they have a helicopter to take her to a hospital? Or had they changed their mind and would let her go?

There were sounds as if Rosa was kicking and punching and shouting and screaming.

My stomach clenched, and my heart thumped in my chest.

Moments later, Rosa's struggles went silent, and the whispers started up again before footsteps pounded down the hall until I could hear nothing at all.

9

MARTINA

LEANING AGAINST THE WALL OF THE COLD CASE SQUAD room, I nodded as Vincent told us the latest update. Blaine hadn't taken out any large life insurance policies on his wife. The only policy on Sadie was the standard one through her work. The financials on Blaine couldn't be retrieved, considering we didn't have a warrant to do a deep dive. But the fact there was no life insurance policy on Sadie other than her workplace policy, standard for all the employees at the hospital, made me think if Blaine killed his wife, the motive was something other than financial. "The only other thing I found was the sale of the boat. He received a hefty penny for that. Without being able to look into his bank statements, I'd say he's probably fairly set financially, and his family is wealthy. Prominent. Old money."

"Does Blaine have any siblings?" I asked.

"Two. His brother Marcus lives in San Francisco and works in banking. He has a younger sister. There isn't much about her in the press, and I couldn't find any employment records for her."

"What's her name?"

"Breanna Jarreau. From what I could find, she's a few years younger than Blaine. There are no records of college attendance for her other than one year at the University of San Francisco."

"Maybe she's the black sheep of the family?"

"Maybe. I'll keep digging."

"Good."

"What are you thinking?" Hirsch asked.

I cocked my head. "Just for the sake of argument, let's say Blaine killed Sadie — motive unknown. He plans to go to the boat that day, but he's surprised to see her. He doesn't want her there. They have an argument, and he knocks her overboard, never to be seen again. Maybe it was an accident. Maybe not."

"Or?" Hirsch asked.

"Who else would have a motive to kill or take Sadie?" I asked.

Vincent said, "Maybe it was a kidnapping and ransom gone wrong? She was from a wealthy family."

I said, "That's a good point. Let's go over to Blaine's office and see if he can give us any insight or if he received any ransom notes or if there was any hint of something like that happening to Sadie or anybody in his family. I'd also like to know if he thought she was pregnant. He is a physician."

Hirsch said, "I'd also like to know if he went on the boat that day."

"All right, let's head over to Dr. Jarreau's office. Vincent, we'll see you later."

Vincent said, "I'll keep looking into the sister and try to find what I can about Blaine's finances."

We waved and exited the station. Hirsch said, "Is your gut talking to you yet?"

"Not yet. It has more questions than answers. But it doesn't seem to be a straightforward 'the husband did it.' It's not financially motivated, and everyone says he loved her. Although May said he was having an affair. Maybe he was getting ready to leave Sadie and start a family with a new woman. Finds out Sadie's pregnant, but it's too late."

Hirsch said, "But he had an alibi for that day. He was working at the hospital all night. The original statements verified it."

"Only one other physician verified his alibi. Maybe the other doctor is covering for Blaine, for whatever reason."

"It's possible."

It was possible, but it was also a long shot. But something wasn't right here. I couldn't figure out what it was. It was becoming clear why the case had gone cold so quickly. There wasn't an obvious motive for Sadie's disappearance, only strange coincidences like the cameras on the dock not working that day. Although the camera issues were a known intermittent problem, so it wasn't anything out of the ordinary. Maybe we were making this too complicated. It was usually the husband. The likelihood it was somebody else was a very small percentage.

Suicide didn't seem likely based on what we had heard from both Blaine and May. May, the last person to see her alive, other than Sam in the slip next to the Jarreau boat, said she was upbeat and in a good mood that day. Had Sadie been happy that her life was ending, or was she happy because something good was happening? I wished I knew.

We stood in front of Vicki, the receptionist, once again.

"You're back already?" she asked with an apprehensive smile.

Hirsch said, "Yes, I'm hoping we can have a few minutes of Dr. Jarreau's time. We won't be long."

"Let me go check in with him. I'll be right back." She swiveled her chair and hurried toward the medical offices.

At least everyone we'd talked to so far had been cooperative, considering our last big case, when half of our witnesses either wouldn't talk to us or ended up dead. I didn't need another one of those cases for a while, thank you very much. New year, new attitude.

We didn't always have to run into the fire. We could solve some of the lower hanging fruit for us to catch our breath and make sure we got Hirsch and Kim married and on their honeymoon without a hitch.

The door opened, and Dr. Jarreau said, "Come in, Detective and Ms. Monroe."

He didn't look as shaken as he had the day before. Was it because he'd had time to prepare his statements for us? He was smart, and that was what he should be doing. Back in his office, he said, "What can I do for you?"

I said, "We have a few follow-up questions for you based on a couple of interviews we did yesterday. First, did you know the day that Sadie disappeared, your boat was taken out of the harbor and returned by the next morning?"

The color drained from Blaine's face. "Nobody ever told me that."

"Did you meet Sadie that night and go out on the boat with her?" Hirsch asked.

"No, I didn't. I swear it."

"Do you know who did?" I asked.

He shook his head vigorously. "No, this is all very surprising." He fidgeted before sitting down in his desk chair. "But the cameras weren't working that day. How did you know?"

I raised a brow. "How did you know the cameras weren't working that day?"

"The first detective to investigate her disappearance told me."

Studying his face, I tried to determine if he was lying. He was certainly flustered. Why?

"One of your neighbors at the marina saw Sadie that day. He also saw that the boat went out but had returned by morning. Do you think Sadie would have taken the boat out by herself?"

"No, I don't. I don't think she knows how to drive the boat. It's not as easy as people think. And the few times she'd gone out with me, I drove. I offered to teach her, but she didn't want to learn."

Somebody had to have been with her that day. "Is there anybody you can think of who may have wanted to harm Sadie?"

"No. Sadie was special. She's kind and full of empathy. Smart and really cared about other people. It's why she became a nurse. I can't imagine anybody would want to hurt her, ever," he said, with tears forming in his eyes.

If I didn't know any better, I'd say that he, in fact, loved Sadie. If his words about her were true, she was a good person, and he didn't want to hurt her and nobody else who knew her did either.

"We've heard that your family comes from money. Any way this could have been a kidnapping and ransom gone wrong?" Hirsch asked.

"I thought of that. If that was the plan, I never got a ransom call or note."

There went that theory. "Before Sadie went missing, was she acting normal? Did she have a change in energy, habits, routines, or exercise schedules?"

The doctor cocked his head as if trying to remember five years ago, before she went missing. "Well, she seemed tired, I guess. I once made a comment that she looked like she needed a nap. She had dark circles under her eyes. I just assumed the long hours at work were getting to her." Something in his eyes changed — maybe recognition that he might have missed something.

"May said she had been tired and was munching on crackers quite a bit."

Dr. Jarreau bowed his head and mumbled, "Oh my God."

"Did you know your wife was pregnant?" I asked.

He lifted his head. "You know she was pregnant?"

Odd question. "No, we don't know for sure. It was a theory May had. It could've been something else. But you didn't know she was pregnant, if she was pregnant?"

He shook his head. "No, I didn't know. I wish I had known," he said sadly.

"You know she was out on the boat that day to meet you and surprise you with dinner?"

"That's what I heard."

"May said you told Sadie you were going there after work and that's why Sadie went there."

"I had planned to go out on the boat, forgetting I had a shift at the hospital that night. I wish she would've called me instead of making it a surprise. If she would've called, I could've met her somewhere else. Or I could have changed shifts at the hospital, and we could've been together."

Blaine stared out the window, shaking his head as if filled with regret at how things had turned out. I wished I could get a better read on him. My gut was screaming this man had loved his wife, but it wasn't telling me he was innocent. Maybe it was an argument, and an accident had occurred. Maybe that's where the guilt and regret were coming from. We thanked Dr. Jarreau for his time and made our way out of the medical office.

Walking out into the brisk air, I wrapped my scarf around my neck and zipped up my jacket. Hirsch gave me a look like he was as puzzled as I was. "Let's go talk to the Coast Guard to verify there weren't any reported sightings of the boat the night Sadie went missing and then also double-check Blaine's alibi at the hospital. If it really wasn't him there that night, I'd like to confirm that before hunting for an unknown person."

After saluting Hirsch, I said, "Aye, aye, captain."

10

MARTINA

HE EXTENDED HIS MEATY HAND AND SMILED. "CAPTAIN Jack Powder at your service, ma'am."

"I appreciate that, sir. Martina Monroe."

"Am I sensing former military?"

"Army."

He winked. "I suppose that's okay."

I couldn't help but smile. He was ruggedly handsome, with a five o'clock shadow and shoulder-length salt-and-pepper hair blowing in the wind.

After Hirsch introduced himself, we walked into Captain Jack Powder's office. "What can I do for you two?" he asked.

"We have reopened the cold case of a missing woman, Sadie Jarreau. She was last seen at the Alameda marina. We received new information that one of her neighbors at slip 16 saw her that day and then later saw the boat missing, presumably out to sea, but then the boat was docked again by morning. He didn't see when she left or when the boat returned. We're hoping to learn from you if there were any reported sightings of the boat that night."

"I can check, but I have to warn you. There may not be a

record, but that doesn't mean the boat didn't go out. We only get reports of distress calls or suspicious activity."

I said, "Understood."

Jack nodded and turned his attention to the computer screen.

This man was interesting to me. I couldn't deny I was attracted to him, and that made me feel weird inside. Even weirder that I had agreed to let Kim set me up with a college friend of hers. The timing of the date was to be determined until I talked to Zoey about it. I would only go on the date if Zoey was okay with me going out with another man. Even though I knew her memories of her father were fading, Zoey was my world, and I had to make sure it would not disrupt her young life. If she was against it, I didn't need to go on a date, not yet. I was curious about dating again, but I could be patient too.

Jack returned his focus to us. "I checked the logs from that night. No records of any communication with the boat number you gave me. But like I said, that doesn't mean it wasn't out cruising around. Do you know where it was going?"

I said, "That's the thing. We don't know who was with Sadie on the boat, and we don't know where they were going. All we know is that it went out and came back, and Sadie was never seen again."

Jack leaned back in his chair and crossed his arms. "You know, I remember this case."

"You do?" Hirsch asked.

"Yes, because shortly after she went missing, we caught a floater. I was with the team that retrieved the body. We were for sure thinking it was Sadie. The doctor's wife, right?"

"Yes, and she was a nurse."

Jack nodded. "Yeah, but it wasn't her. We knew right away because the woman, although badly decomposed, had characteristics that didn't match Sadie's."

"And what were those characteristics?"

"Well, for starters, the body was Hispanic. Dark hair. Brown skin. And the woman had been pregnant — and had recently given birth — like a few days before death. The baby was never found."

A shiver ran down my spine. Who would murder a woman days after she had given birth? "The baby was never found?"

"The theory at the time was that they had taken the woman for the child. Once the child was born, the perpetrators killed the woman and dumped her body into the bay."

Thinking back five years, I didn't recall hearing about the death on the news. Something so grim, so sinister, surely would have made national news. Come to think of it, I didn't recall hearing about Sadie's disappearance, either. That was strange, considering she was from a prominent family or had married into one. "I don't recall hearing about it in the news. Do you, Hirsch?"

"No."

"Don't you remember what was dominating the headlines at the time?" Jack asked with a knowing grin.

"Five years ago... was that..."

Jack nodded. "A pretty, white, pregnant woman went missing on the Fourth of July. The only thing the news covered that summer was that case. She remained on the news until her body was found in the bay with her baby still in the womb. They arrested the husband for it. Basically, if you weren't more sympathetic than a pretty, white, pregnant woman, you weren't making the news."

The woman whose baby had been stolen, and then her body discarded, and Sadie, a caring, empathetic nurse weren't worthy of the news because they didn't meet the criteria for public interest? I shook my head in disappointment at mankind. "Did they ever find out what happened to the Hispanic woman whose baby had been stolen?"

"As far as I know, they never solved the case. One clever journalist thought maybe this white woman was taken by the same people who killed the Hispanic woman and had found other missing persons under similar circumstances. Young, pregnant, and missing. But when they nabbed the husband for the white women's murder, they dropped the idea of a connection. Nobody ever cared to look into the other young, pregnant, Hispanic women who went missing around the same time."

I exhaled and thought about that. Here we were searching for another white woman when there were so many other missing persons who didn't get the same attention because they were a different color or had a different economic background. It wasn't fair. The realization didn't help our case, but it was something to think about. I would have to talk to Hirsch about maybe adding some diversity to which cold cases we reopened. Sometimes, we didn't have a choice, like when the sheriff told us what we would work on and when we wanted to help Vincent and his girlfriend's family. But other times, we had a choice.

WE HAD BEEN ON THE MOVE FOR SEVERAL DAYS, AND IT HAD been several weeks since they took Rosa. I didn't know where she went, but she never returned. I had been a prisoner in this massive suite for so long my muscles were stiffening, so I had started doing jumping jacks, push-ups, and sit-ups to keep in shape. I was well fed but lacking sunshine and fresh air. This wasn't a way to live.

Heavy footsteps sounded.

Were they coming for me?

There were multiple people going into the other state room without a word. They shut the door and the footfall neared my own.

My heart beat fast.

Three knocks and my door opened. It was the man and that woman with the dark hair and green eyes who had been on the boat when we first boarded. "Sadie, we have a proposition for you."

A proposition? "What is it?"

"We'd like to give you more freedom to walk around the

deck and enjoy the sunshine and ocean views, but we need something in return."

"What is it? I'll do anything." Well, not *anything*.

"We know that you're a nurse and seemed to have a way with Rosa. We have a new visitor. Her name is Janine, and we were thinking maybe you could help her. She's just hit her seventh month of pregnancy, and she's having twins. We think you could look after her, and in return, we'll let you have free roam of the upper deck, which has a small kitchenette stocked with snacks and beverages and a nice walking track. The chef, of course, will continue to provide your main meals. What do you say?"

What's the catch? And how did they know I was a nurse? Were there news stories about my disappearance? Surely, they must have found my car at the marina. The woman's green eyes bore into my soul. "Okay."

She nodded. "Excellent. Why don't you come with us, so you can meet Janine. We'll introduce the two of you and explain you'll be her caretaker and will keep her and the babies safe."

"What happened to Rosa?"

The woman sighed. "It would be best if you didn't ask questions."

"Okay." *For now.* I was still a prisoner but given some freedom. I would need to figure out how to use that to my advantage. "Do you have medical supplies? Twins can be complicated." But then again, even if I tried to run, where would I go? I was on a boat in the middle of the ocean. I had no idea where we were.

"We have medical supplies on board. We have basic first-aid products down here, but down the hall, we have more specialized equipment."

More specialized equipment? Specialized for what?

Forcing myself to appear grateful and eager to please, I said,

"Great. After I meet Janine, may I go up to the deck to get some sunshine?"

My baby and I needed it.

She said, "Not yet. There will be certain hours you'll be permitted on the main deck. I'll provide you with a schedule."

So, not total freedom. "Thank you."

She smiled. "Let's go meet Janine."

I nodded as my belly flip-flopped. I wasn't sure if it was the baby or my nerves. The woman, two men, and I trekked down the hall until we hit the far end of the yacht. The woman opened the door and there, sitting on the bench, was a woman with chestnut hair, brown eyes, and freckles across the bridge of her nose. She was quite pregnant. If I hadn't already known she was having twins, I would have guessed it.

The woman with green eyes said, "Janine, this is Sadie, and she's going to take care of you. She'll make sure that you and your babies are healthy, okay?"

"Why are you doing this?" Janine cried.

"Now, we've talked about this. It's best that there aren't questions. We ask the questions. We give the orders. Not you. Do you understand?"

Janine nodded as tears streamed down her cheeks.

I said, "It's nice to meet you, Janine," as guilt filled me up. Had I made a deal with the devil? Sure, if we were in a hospital and this woman hadn't been kidnapped, it would be nice to meet a new person. But Janine's current circumstances weren't anything I would wish upon anyone.

The woman said, "I'll leave you two to get acquainted. We'll allow you to roam around this deck, but don't cross the gate up to the upper deck without permission or there will be consequences. Severe consequences. Do you both understand?"

"Yes."

Janine said, "Yeah, I get it."

The dark-haired woman and her two soldiers stepped out of the room, and the door slammed shut. I sat on the bench across from Janine. "I'm so sorry that this is happening to you. They took me too."

"They did? You aren't one of them?"

I shook my head. "No. I arrived on my boat to surprise my husband with a special dinner, and I found another woman, another pregnant woman, tied up, and then those men with the guns came in. Now I'm here."

"What happened to the other woman?"

Staring into her pleading eyes, I said, "I don't know. They told me not to ask what happened to her." Any speculation I had wouldn't help Janine in her current condition.

Janine cried uncontrollably. She only stopped long enough to say, "They're going to kill me and steal my babies."

Sliding off the bench, I went over to the bed to comfort Janine as she cried. I didn't know what I could say to make the situation better. Janine's fate was probably no better than Rosa's. Was there anything we could do to stop them?

We were in the middle of nowhere, and they had weapons. Maybe I could get ahold of the radio and send a signal that we needed help. Once they let me up on the main deck, I would have time to look around and see if there was anything I could use to our advantage. I hopped off the bed and went into the bathroom to pull out some tissues and bring them back to Janine.

She accepted them and dried her eyes and blew her nose. "You're really not one of them?"

I shook my head again. "I don't know why they took me or what they're going to do with me. But I am a nurse, and they've asked me to take care of you in exchange for a little freedom. We won't be stuck in one room, which I welcome. I've been in my room for weeks."

"I'm so sorry. Are you pregnant, too?"

Looking into her eyes, I did something I never thought I would. "No, I'm not. I think it was just the wrong place, wrong time kind of thing for me."

I didn't know Janine, and I felt sorry for her and her situation, but I didn't want her telling them I was pregnant. After what I suspected they had done with Rosa, and would do with Janine, I wouldn't allow them to find out I was pregnant too.

12

HIRSCH

LEANING ON THE HOOD OF MY CAR, I LOOKED BACK AT THE hospital. The records department and a few of the doctors we'd questioned had confirmed Jarreau's alibi. Security even showed us footage from the night Sadie disappeared. Clear as day, we watched as Blaine entered the hospital, and then in the early hours of the next morning, he exited. That was what we called an air-tight alibi.

Blaine couldn't have been the person with Sadie the night she disappeared, assuming she'd been with anybody. It wasn't beyond reasonable doubt that she could have taken the boat out by herself, but it made little sense if she had. In my experience, the more logical things were, the more likely they were true. We needed to figure out who Sadie was with that night because they were most likely the person responsible for her disappearance.

We would be lucky to get security footage from the surrounding area near the marina. Maybe a few blocks away, some suspicious folks would be caught on film. It was a stretch considering it was five years ago and most people and organizations only kept security tapes for a certain number of days, weeks, or months. Rarely longer. I had nearly fainted when the hospital security said they kept their tapes for seven years. Something to do with medical records retention policies. It was unusual, but it had alibied Blaine Jarreau. That didn't mean he couldn't have hired someone to kill Sadie. But that was unlikely, too. The fact that Sadie's decision to go to the boat that day wasn't planned ahead of time, and Blaine didn't know about it, made it unlikely to have been a planned attack.

I wondered if Sadie's disappearance was one of the rare stranger abductions that occurred. It wasn't beyond belief that she could have been that unlucky. Perhaps wrong place, wrong time. Maybe she witnessed something she shouldn't have. But what?

There wasn't a lot of crime reported in the Alameda marina area, but that didn't mean it didn't happen. Boats were great ways to smuggle drugs and people. All the witnesses had said that nothing strange had happened that day and that it was a relatively quiet afternoon, evening, and morning. If there had been a big drug deal, somebody would have remembered.

There was something bothering me about our conversation with the Coast Guard. What if the body of the formerly pregnant woman and Sadie's disappearance were connected? What if Sadie had seen something?

The timeline of the body being discovered and Sadie's disappearance was less than a week. I hadn't been a big believer in coincidences before, and I hadn't started yet.

Martina said, "Head back to the station?"

"Yep."

"Did you think they wouldn't alibi him?"

"A little surprised, but it is what it is."

"Maybe he didn't do anything to his wife," she said, less than convincing.

"Don't you think he's hiding something?"

"Yes, but what he's hiding may have absolutely nothing to do with Sadie. Or it could have everything to do with Sadie. Maybe whatever he's hiding was what led to her demise?"

"Maybe."

On the way back to the station, I said, "I hear you and Zoey have plans with Kim tomorrow night to try on Zoey's flower girl dress."

"All Zoey can talk about is your wedding and the frilly pink dress she gets to wear and how she's gonna do her hair, and she's even angling for me to allow her to wear lip gloss."

"It'll be quite the day."

"You getting nervous?" Martina asked.

"About getting married?"

She nodded.

"No. I've never been this certain about anything. Kim's it for me."

"That's great, Hirsch."

"Have you talked to Zoey about your blind date?" I asked, wondering if she'd had the conversation with Zoey yet. I knew *all the details,* courtesy of Kim. She was excited to set up Martina with one of her friends from college. Kim told me she wasn't sure if they would be a love match, but he was a nice man, and maybe he would show Martina that there were other nice men out there. But I knew Martina would never do anything to hurt Zoey, and if Zoey wasn't okay with her dating, she wouldn't. I had been around Zoey enough over the last two years to believe she would be happy for her mother to start dating. She was a special kid and wise beyond her ten years. I hoped any child Kim and I brought into this world would have a similar sparkle, intelligence, and pizzazz for life. If he or she did, they would surely inherit it from Kim.

"Not yet. I was thinking of calling Kim and asking her if she didn't mind if I talked to Zoey about it tomorrow night."

"It's not a conversation you want to have with just the two of you?"

"That was what I was originally thinking, but Zoey idolizes Kim, and I think maybe Kim is unbiased enough to help us through the conversation if it gets difficult."

"I'm sure Kim would be happy to provide backup. Just call her."

"I will."

Before we made it through the doors of the CoCo County Sheriff's Department, we bumped into Vincent in the parking lot. "Hey, Vincent, what's up? You heading home?"

His eyes were wide. "No way. I just have to grab something from my car, but I have some news for the two of you."

"Oh, yeah?" I asked.

"Let me grab my charger from the car, and I'll meet you back in the squad room. You'll want to hear what I found."

"Okay."

Vincent ran off, and I wondered what he had discovered. Perhaps he had found Blaine's elusive sister or a potential motive for Blaine.

"What do you think that's about?" Martina asked.

"Your guess is as good as mine."

Before we knew it, Vincent was behind us once again. He said, "Okay, so I found something really interesting. When you told me about how they thought Sadie had been the body they retrieved out of the bay the week after she disappeared, you got me thinking."

"And?" Martina asked.

"I did some digging. And not just in the San Francisco Bay Area but up and down the west coast, looking for similar cases of pregnant women gone missing or killed with their babies missing. Well, spoiler. There's far more than you'd ever expect, but I narrowed it down to those women who had been dumped in bodies of water. I found a few with similar characteristics to the one they found the week after Sadie went missing. There were two more women found before her. Her name was Rosa Ruiz. The two before her were called Elsa Alvarez and Catherine Chester. All three were in the last weeks of their pregnancy when they were reported missing. All three found washed ashore, babies MIA."

Stopping, I turned to Martina and Vincent. "Where were the women from?"

"That's the thing. One is from San Leandro, one is from Antioch, and one is from Bakersfield. And last, one was *almost* taken from San Jose."

"What do you mean, almost taken?" I asked.

"A woman eight months pregnant was nearly taken, but when she screamed, the perpetrators ran off."

"Three killed and one attempted kidnapping. All eight to nine months pregnant?" Martina asked incredulously.

"That's right. All reported missing from different counties and found in different bodies of water. Pacifica, Berkeley, and San Francisco Bay. None of the departments talk to each other. None of them made the news."

Martina said, "What's the timeframe?"

"They found the first three over a two-year span, starting six years ago. The three women went missing three months apart. Almost exactly."

"Anything since then?"

"I'm still looking, but that means..."

Martina cut him off. "There's a serial killer out there targeting pregnant women and stealing their babies."

The three of us stood there in silence.

Could this have anything to do with Sadie's disappearance? There was speculation she may have been pregnant. But at the time she went missing, she couldn't have been more than three or four months along, and nobody knew for sure she was pregnant, so she probably wasn't a target. But it seemed too close to home.

I said, "Okay, Vincent, I want the names and addresses of the family members of all the women, especially the woman who was almost taken in San Jose. I'm not sure it's a connection to Sadie or not, but either way, it needs our attention."

"No kidding," Martina added.

"You got it, boss."

I returned to the Cold Case Squad room with a million thoughts running through my mind. Had we just stumbled into another serial killer situation? And was there a connection to Sadie? If not, so be it. Somebody needed to find out what happened to those women and their children. If for no other reason than to make sure it didn't happen to any others.

13

MARTINA

A MAN WITH DARK HAIR, WEATHERED SKIN, AND SAD EYES welcomed Hirsch and me into his home. "This is my wife, Maria."

"It's nice to meet you, Maria. My name is Martina, and this is my partner Detective Hirsch."

"It's nice to meet you. Thank you for not giving up on Elsa. She deserves justice like everybody else."

"Yes, she does. Please, let's all sit," I said.

Seated, Maria continued to clutch her rosary. "I'm so grateful that you are looking into Elsa's case. Have you found something new? Is that the reason you are here?"

"While we were investigating the disappearance of a woman, it was brought to our attention that other women had been found where she was last seen alive. One of those women was Elsa and two others with similar circumstances. All three women found had been eight to nine months pregnant when they were reported missing, and their bodies were later found without their babies."

"Who would do that?" Maria asked.

"We don't know. But we're hoping to find out more about

Elsa before she went missing to help us figure out what may have happened. We will also talk to the other women's families to see if there are additional similarities between the women. We're hoping to find a connection that could lead us to who's responsible for their deaths."

Mr. Alvarez said, "I understand."

My heart beat faster as I asked questions about their deceased daughter and missing grandchild. They were questions I never wanted to have to ask and hoped to God they would never ask me those same questions. "Please tell us about Elsa. What she was like, who her friends were, and about the father of the baby."

Mr. Alvarez said something in Spanish that I couldn't understand, but I was fairly certain they were kind words. Maria put her hand on her husband's. "Elsa was wonderful, caring, loving, trusting. She went to school, high school. She was only eighteen when she disappeared. At first, when she told us about the pregnancy, we weren't thrilled. Elsa had planned to go to college. The first one in our family. Children are a blessing, but we really hoped that Elsa would've waited for that blessing. She was so smart..." Maria teared up.

Mr. Alvarez bowed his head. He looked back up at me. "So smart. Funny too. At first, we were upset about the pregnancy, but once we got used to the idea, we decided Elsa would stay home with us, and we would help her raise the baby so she could continue to go to school. She liked the idea, and we grew to love the baby growing inside of her. It was going to be a little boy, my grandson."

The pain radiating off Mr. Alvarez was palpable.

"I'm sorry for your loss. I can't imagine what you're going through, but my partner and I will try to find out what happened to Elsa and your grandson."

Hirsch said, "What can you tell us about the father of the baby?"

Maria shook her head. "He was no good. He was handsome and had a fancy car. You know the kind. He didn't go to school. I tried to warn Elsa. He was a little older and was her first actual boyfriend. We didn't care for him, but for the sake of our grandson and our daughter, we tried to be welcoming."

"What was his name?"

Maria said, "Hector Martinez. He lives here in Antioch. I'm pretty sure he still lives with his mother."

I glanced at Hirsch, who was writing the name in his notebook. "Do you have any reason to believe Hector may have had something to do with Elsa's disappearance?"

"I wouldn't put it past him to do something terrible, but he swore he didn't know what happened to her. When her body was found, he acted upset but more like surprised upset. The police questioned him, but apparently, he had an alibi. They said he wasn't a suspect anymore."

"Had anybody been harassing Elsa, or did she tell you about any strange encounters leading up to her disappearance?"

Maria said, "She said people were really friendly with her and always wanting to touch her belly. She couldn't stand it. She said it's my body, my rules. Right before she disappeared, Elsa told us one woman was very aggressive and tried to get her to tell her all about the baby like the sex, due date, and how involved the father was. It spooked her."

That aggressive questioning was odd. But I remembered being pregnant with Zoey and strangers always wanting to touch my belly and thinking they had the right to. *They didn't.* I didn't mind if someone asked politely or seemed friendly, but it would be awfully off-putting if somebody had been aggressive and demanding answers about the father of my child. "Did she tell you anything else about this woman who had been aggressive?"

"Just that it was some strange white lady."

"Where was Elsa last seen?" Hirsch asked.

"She was at the bus stop on her way home from school. Somebody took her."

"Were there any witnesses?" Hirsch asked.

I'd read the case file, and since Elsa was last seen in and was from CoCo County and a cold case, it was ours. And that was why we visited Elsa's family first. It was the closest, and we had all the paperwork in hand. Upon review of the files, it was no surprise the investigation lacked genuine effort.

"A few people said they saw a van pull up, and they pushed her inside. It was a white van. No license plate."

"Anything else you can tell us about Elsa that might help us find out what happened to her?" Hirsch asked.

"No."

"Have you received any strange phone calls or messages?" I asked.

They shook their heads.

We stood up from the couch. "Mr. and Mrs. Alvarez, thank you for speaking with us. We will keep you updated as we progress in the investigation. We just reopened the case this week, so it might take us some time, but we won't give up on getting justice for you and Elsa and your grandson."

"Thank you."

We saw ourselves out of the house. These interviews were tough and emotionally draining. How could anybody take a young mother and steal her baby and then discard her into the water? What was the motive? I could only think of one.

Within the confines of the car, I said, "Do you know of any trafficking rings that may be in the baby selling business?"

"I haven't heard of any in my time in law enforcement, but

I'm sure they exist. It would make sense if they were behind the killings of these women. If it were just one woman, it may be a different story — like a weirdo with a fetish for pregnant women. But there's three. That's likely for profit."

"Some guy with a pregnant woman fetish would be easier to find than who may have taken these women and their babies."

Hirsch nodded. "I agree. A trafficking ring, or some form of organized crime, targeting young pregnant women from underserved populations and spacing them out among counties to avoid detection... sounds like professionals to me."

"In other words, a sophisticated set of criminals, not one bad guy, but possibly many bad guys."

That was not good news. In my experience, organized crime didn't just stop after a few deals. We may not find any more bodies washing ashore in the San Francisco Bay Area, but that didn't mean they had stopped taking pregnant women and their babies. This was much bigger than finding Sadie Jarreau. This was about finding a group of criminals murdering young women and stealing their infants. Sadie's disappearance wasn't similar to those of the pregnant women who had died, but my gut was telling me there was some connection. I just wasn't sure what. But I felt confident if we could find out who took those pregnant women, we'd be one step closer to finding out what happened to Sadie.

14

MARTINA

As we approached the home of Ariana Embree, I hoped she could give us more information than the last two victims' families. Elsa's family said there was an aggressive white woman talking to her nonstop and wanting to touch her belly days before she was abducted and then later killed. Catherine's family had spoken with us over the phone and told us Catherine had mentioned no strange encounters before she went missing and the father of the baby was incarcerated several months before her disappearance. He was still locked up. Catherine had simply vanished when she had run out to pick up milk from the grocery store.

We had one more family to visit in Bakersfield, but it was quite a drive, and Ariana Embree was local. Hopefully, Ariana could give us some valuable information to help us narrow down who we were looking for. My biggest concern wasn't whether we could catch the criminals but if the sheriff's department would let us go to the lengths necessary to do so. With each passing minute, I contemplated how to justify a large-scale investigation that would likely need to involve several jurisdictions. The pregnant women's case was top priority in my mind, but that didn't mean we would stop looking for Sadie.

Hirsch knocked on the door. A man with a thick mustache and cheerful brown eyes said, "You must be the detective and the investigator?"

"Yes, my name is Detective Hirsch, and this is my partner, Ms. Monroe. May we come in?"

"Yes, I'm so sorry. My name is Mack Embree, Ariana's father. She's with my wife in the living room with our grandson."

"Thank you."

Mack let us into the sitting room where a middle-aged Latina woman and a younger version played with a five-year-old boy. The younger of the two women stood up and extended her hand. "Hi, I'm Ariana."

I said, "It's nice to meet you."

After introductions, I had to pick my jaw off the floor when Hirsch knelt down on one knee to introduce himself to the little boy. "What's your name?"

"Mario," he said sweetly.

"Hi, Mario. My name is Detective Hirsch."

The little boy didn't say anything, but he did smile and make a bit of a noise that sounded like he was trying to contain his excitement. Hirsch pulled out his badge and showed it to him. Mario's eyes lit up. "A policeman."

"That's right, I'm a policeman."

"Cool."

"I was hoping maybe you could hold on to my badge for me while we talked to your mommy and your grandparents."

He nodded vigorously as he clasped the detective shield in his small hands. Mario ran over to his grandpa and showed him.

The scene was pure joy, but it made me sad too. Ariana had been so close to ending up like Elsa, Catherine, and Rosa.

As Hirsch was getting up off the ground, I gave him a look like *we'll talk about this later*. Did Hirsch have babies on his mind? During our last big case, he'd cooed over a baby girl, and now his connection with this little boy was undeniable. If Hirsch wanted to be a father, I thought he'd make a great one.

We sat down across from Ariana and her family. "Thank you for meeting with us. We really appreciate it."

Ariana said, "I'm just glad someone will listen to my story."

"They didn't take the abduction attempt seriously back then?"

Ariana shook her head. "No, they said I was being hysterical. I know what those people wanted. They wanted me to go with them. One even grabbed my arm, but when I screamed, they ran off."

"Can you walk us through the encounter with..." I paused and glanced over at Mario, who was still fully entranced by Hirsch's badge. "The people who tried to take you."

Ariana nodded. "I was working at a grocery store. It wasn't very busy that day, and I'd only had a few customers. This woman came in and started chatting me up about the baby. When I was due, that kind of thing. I first thought she was being friendly, but then this other man came up behind her. She gave him this look like... I don't know. She nodded like it was some sort of signal to do it. You know what I mean?"

I said, "I think I do."

"And then the man grabbed my arm and dragged me toward the front of the store. The woman trailed behind, but when we were steps away from the door, I screamed and screamed and screamed. He let go of my arm, and the pair ran off. I think it was because there were people right outside the door. The doors are glass, so I could see."

Whoever was outside the store that day saved her life and Mario's.

"What did you do next?" Hirsch asked.

"I called the police. I was so scared. But when they arrived, they told me I was being dramatic, and that it wasn't likely a real abduction attempt."

"Did they say why?" I asked.

"They said if they were serious about taking me, they would have a weapon and that they likely were on drugs or something. I know what people are like when they're on drugs. Those two weren't. And after they found that woman's body with no baby inside, I knew that was what the couple was after. I thank God every day that I screamed and that those people were there because I know without a doubt that would've been my fate."

She wasn't wrong. "Do you remember what the man and woman looked like?"

"Yes. The woman had short, light blonde hair. Medium height."

"Was it a platinum blonde or more of a yellow?"

"Not platinum, warmer blonde. Not natural. Definitely a dye job."

"Eye color?" Hirsch asked.

"Blue. She definitely had blue eyes. Blonde-haired lady with blue eyes. Not somebody you would suspect to be a kidnapper, you know?"

"What can you tell us about the man who grabbed you?"

"Tall, maybe six feet, maybe a little taller. Muscular, with dark hair and dark eyes, but a white guy, though."

"Any tattoos or an accent or anything that would distinguish them?"

"I didn't see any tattoos or anything like that. But our neighborhood is mostly Latino. These people didn't belong there, you know, blonde-haired, blue-eyed, skinny, average height lady and a big man. I knew it was off."

"Did the police ever follow up with you after the other woman's body was recovered?"

"No, the only time anybody ever followed up was the news reporter. Somehow, he got a copy of the report of my attempted abduction. They pulled the records and came to talk to me about it. Not that it helped catch the people who did it."

My gut said it was not a coincidence that Elsa talked about an aggressive white woman and Ariana described a white woman and a white man who had tried to abduct her.

"Did you ever see the couple again?"

"No, never again, but I also stopped working there after the incident. I was too upset to be there again."

I can only imagine. Glancing over at Mario, still proudly holding the detective shield in his hands and sitting next to his grandpa on the sofa, I said, "You were smart to call out for help, and I think you got very lucky."

"I hope you find them. People like that are bad, and they don't suddenly become good. Who knows how many other women and babies they've stolen?"

My thoughts exactly.

We said our goodbyes and Hirsch retrieved his detective shield from the little boy. It was sobering to listen to Ariana's account of her near abduction and likely murder. There was someone looking out for her and Mario that day.

Back in the car, I said, "What did you make of that?"

"There is enough to speculate that the couple who tried to take Ariana is most likely responsible for the other women's deaths. The tricky part will be to identify and then find them."

"No kidding. Do you think it's enough to get a statewide task force together? There's no way these criminals aren't operating up and down the coast."

"I hope so. With all the women we have found who died in the same manner and were dumped the same way, I think it's in the best interest of the state to keep our pregnant women safe and ensure their babies stay with their families."

"Yep."

"I'll set up some time with Sarge and maybe the sheriff, so we can talk about initiating a task force along with the other counties in California. I agree with Ariana. These people are bad, and they're probably still doing bad things to pregnant women and God knows who else. They need to be stopped."

Don't I know it?

15

HIRSCH

THINKING ABOUT MARIO, I ENVISIONED MY SON BEING enamored with the detective's badge. I couldn't wait to marry Kim and for us to try for our own family. Just a few years ago, I'd thought I would remain single and my life dedicated to being a cop and was so sure it was all I needed. But recently, I wondered if in reality I would have ended up sad and alone, in an empty house, with no children — just cop buddies and Zoey. Zoey was a fantastic kid, and she was part of the reason I could envision having my own child. My entire world had changed when I met Kim, and I was so glad it did. Had I grown soft in my old age? If I had, I was okay with it.

We pulled up to the station, and Martina said, "Penny for your thoughts?"

"Just thinking about stuff."

She snorted, as if she knew exactly what I was thinking about. After she calmed herself, she said, "Is that so? What things, Hirsch?"

"Just about the future and Kim and me and..."

Before I could finish, she said, "And a little Hirsch and a little Kim? I saw how you looked at baby Emily from the Twin

Satan Murder case and how you were with Mario just now. You're going to make a great dad."

"I hope so."

Martina grew serious.

"Don't get all misty on me now."

"I can't help it. I'm overjoyed for you and Kim, and a baby..."

"She's not pregnant yet." And hearing about the struggles the Jarreau's had getting pregnant, I knew conceiving a child wasn't a given.

"She will be. I can see it. Oh, Hirsch, I couldn't be happier."

"Well, don't jinx it. Don't say anything to anybody else. But yes, Kim and I plan to start a family shortly after the wedding. Neither one of us is getting any younger. I'm excited and can't wait to have my own little boy or girl in my arms."

"It can be tough with the job we have."

"I can see that. I see you and Zoey and how much your mom helps out. But, you know, things could change too."

"What do you mean?" Martina asked.

"I mean I love the job, and it's what I was meant to do, but family is so important. I think I would put the family first, even if it meant changing jobs."

Martina was silent.

"What's the matter?" I asked.

"I think that's really smart and brave. I feel like I haven't always put my family first. What if something happened to me? Zoey would be an orphan. Having a dangerous job puts that in jeopardy."

"I think you're being too hard on yourself, Martina. You work tirelessly for the job, the victims, and the families, but you still prioritize being there for Zoey. Her Girl Scout meetings. Your Friday night movie nights. Walking in the park with Zoey and Barney. Zoey's school events. You're an amazing mom."

"That's now. I didn't always. Now I try to make sure it stays that way. She's ten, and I feel like I'm going to blink and she'll be off to college. Or seeking world domination, whichever comes first."

I chuckled. "It's a toss-up which will happen first. But seriously, I think you're being too hard on yourself. This job is demanding, and it is a calling. I don't think you should feel bad that you have a dangerous job."

"Really? Some criticize me and say I should be more careful, being her only living parent. Sometimes I agree, but other times, I want to show her that women can have tough jobs too."

"I admit when I first met you, I thought you were a little reckless. But you've changed. Since you've been part of the Cold Case Squad, you are there for Zoey, and you are more cautious, like always wearing your vest and waiting for backup when we're pursuing suspects. Although if you could somehow get people to stop shooting at you, I'd appreciate that."

She cracked a smile. "I'm trying. You're right, I am more cautious than before. I can't change the past, but you're right, I need to put my family first."

"I think you already do."

"Thanks."

Inside the squad room, Vincent greeted us. "Just got the background on Blaine's sister."

"And?"

"The sister's name is Breanna Jarreau, and she's got a rap sheet as long as my arm. Assault, petty theft, fraud, and embezzlement. She's done time — federal time."

"You're kidding?"

"Nope."

No wonder Blaine no longer spoke to his sister. They came from prestige and money. Blaine was a physician, and his brother was a big-time banker. Breanna was clearly the black sheep of the family. "You have a last known address?"

"I do. I've also got the name and information for her parole officer."

"Is she still on parole?"

"No, but her PO might know where she's at."

We sat down at the conference table. Vincent joined us. It was worth a shot. I dialed the number to Breanna Jarreau's parole officer.

"Hello, Carla Denton here."

"Hi, my name is Detective Hirsch, with the CoCo County Sheriff's Department. I have a question for you about one of your parolees, Breanna Jarreau. I can spell the name for you if it helps."

"No need. I remember Breanna. A real piece of work."

"How so?"

"She's one of those poor little rich girls who decides all the privilege and family money isn't enough. Plus, she's got a temper — and a real mean streak."

"Not warm and fuzzy?"

The PO laughed. "Not even a little. What did she do this time?"

"Nothing that we know of. Her sister-in-law went missing five years ago, and we're hoping to find her and talk to her about the case."

"Did you try her brother? He's a doctor, if I remember correctly. She used to brag about him all the time."

"Really? Her brother said they haven't kept in touch over the years."

"Six years ago, when she was on my list, he paid all of her bills. Good for him for finally cutting her off."

"No idea where she's at?"

"No. Her last known details went stale the day she was off parole."

"She could be anywhere."

"Yes, sir."

"Well, thanks. You've been helpful."

"Good luck, Detective."

Turning to Martina, I said, "No luck."

"Should we call Blaine and ask him a second time if he knows where she is?"

"It's worth a shot. Maybe now that we have more information about her, Blaine will be more forthcoming."

Martina nodded, and I dialed.

Blaine answered right away. "Hello."

Background noise sounded like he was in an airport. "Blaine, this is Detective Hirsch. Did I catch you at a bad time?"

"I'm at the airport, but I have a few minutes."

"Where are you going?"

"A medical conference."

"Where?"

"Seattle, Washington. What can I do for you?" he said in a hurried tone.

"We're hoping to find out if you have a last known address or contact information for your sister Breanna."

Blaine didn't answer.

"Dr. Jarreau?"

"I haven't spoken to her in years and don't have her phone number."

"How long has it been since you've spoken to her?"

Pause.

"Dr. Jarreau?"

"I don't know, maybe ten years."

Ten years? Had Breanna lied to her parole officer that Blaine was paying her bills? Or was Blaine lying to us?

"What about your parents? Would they have her contact information?"

"I don't know. Maybe, but I don't think she talks to them either."

"We've learned she's done time for some pretty serious stuff. Do you think Breanna could have had something to do with Sadie's disappearance? Maybe she tried to get some money out of you and something went wrong?"

I waited.

And waited.

I looked over at Martina.

"Dr. Jarreau? Are you still there?"

"Uh, yeah. I was just checking the board for my flight information. What was that?"

"I asked if you thought Breanna could have had something to do with Sadie's disappearance."

"No, I don't think so. Knowing Bree, I bet she's lounging on a beach in Mexico, sipping tequila on someone else's dime."

"Do you know of any way to contact her?"

"No."

"Well, if you find her contact information, please call me."

"Of course. I'm sorry, I have to go."

Before I could speak another word, Blaine hung up the phone. I turned to Martina. "That was weird."

"What's that?"

"He's headed to Washington state for a medical conference."

"That's not too unusual, is it?"

"I guess not. But he says he hasn't heard from his sister in ten years and doesn't think his family has either."

"Ten years?"

Exactly. Something was off about Blaine Jarreau's answers, and I was going to find out what.

16

SADIE

IN THE WEEKS SINCE I'D FIRST MET JANINE, I HAD GOTTEN to know her better. After a day or so, she calmed down, was less hysterical, and I was able to learn her story. The details were peculiar, and she was hesitant to tell me too much. I wondered if she still didn't trust me and thought I was one of them. I didn't blame her. How was she to know for sure? Understandably, considering I wasn't pregnant, they kept me fed, and let me up to the top deck.

As I walked along the deck, I tried to ignore the man with the gun who stood at the helm, making sure I didn't... what? Jump overboard? Steal the life preserver and swim to freedom? *Ridiculous.* All I could do was be grateful that the sun was shining with blue skies, puffy clouds, and crystal blue water. Land was off in the distance, but I did not know where we were. I didn't know if we were in international waters or just off the coast of California. It was cool, with a slight breeze, and under almost any other circumstances, cruising on a luxury yacht in the Pacific Ocean would be like a dream.

But instead, I was being held captive and hadn't spoken to

any of my loved ones in so long. Were they still looking for me? The pit in my stomach knew Rosa was dead.

That splash. That night.

I shuddered.

I was sure it was her, but what did they do with the baby? I couldn't see anything. Whenever they set sail or when they docked, they made sure I was in my room. Surely, it was to conceal the location, but based on the weather, we had to be off the coast of California or Mexico.

A lot of what was happening made little sense to me, but most of all, I didn't understand why they were keeping me and why they were treating me as well as they were. The whole thing was so bizarre that I couldn't have made it up if I had tried. Finishing my last lap, I glanced over at the man who stepped toward me. My time up top was over. When I'd made the deal to take care of Janine, the woman said I could have more freedom, but the schedule sometimes only allowed me above deck for no more than an hour a day. But they had provided me with an iPod to listen to music, which was a pleasant surprise.

In our last exchange, I pleaded with the dark-haired woman to give Janine the same comfort, explaining the exercise would be good for the babies, but she wasn't having any of it. She said it was too risky, and I knew better than to ask questions.

Each time they allowed me up deck, I contemplated what I could do to get out of the situation. They'd never allowed me near the radio, and even if I tried to make a run for it, the man who loomed over me with the gun would surely act quickly to stop me. At that point, a rescue seemed like a moon shot.

I had failed to save Rosa, and I wasn't hopeful I could save Janine. The most I could do was try to make her comfortable. Make sure she was healthy, not that it mattered. I wasn't naïve and knew what was going to happen to her.

The man called out, "Time's up."

I nodded and headed toward the back of the boat and down the stairs to Janine and my quarters. We often referred to it as the dungeon. We had windows but they were covered in a dark film which brought in some light, but it provided little visibility to the outside.

I knocked on Janine's door. She said, "Come in."

It was like we were roommates in college. We were each other's only friends at the moment, and even then, I don't think she trusted me. I wondered if she knew I was holding back information about my pregnancy. She couldn't blame me, though, could she? I opened the door and found her sitting on the bench, reading a novel. "How are you feeling?"

"Like a house, stuck on a boat, and wobbling all the time," she said with a faint smile.

"That's pretty normal. How are the babies?"

"Moving, dancing, and jumping up and down on my bladder."

I grinned. "Sounds like they want to come out."

"I'm sure they do." She glanced down and rubbed her belly. "But I think they're safer in there for now, don't you?"

Her smile was long gone.

Time to work my bedside magic and try to get her mind off her future. "So, you're from San Diego?"

"Yes."

"And what do you do for work?"

"I work as an administrative assistant for a medical device company."

"That sounds like interesting work."

"I liked it. When they took me, I was working in the front yard of my house. My husband was at work. I had just gone on maternity leave the day before. It was early but my doctor said with twins they could come at any time." She sighed. "I never thought it would end like this."

My heart was heavy for her. I knew better than to ask this, but I couldn't help it. Maybe talking about the babies would raise her spirits. "Do you have names picked out for them?"

She nodded. "Jordan for a girl and Thomas for a boy. Of course, we also picked out alternate names for boys and girls since we decided not to find out the sex of the babies until they're born."

"Those are beautiful names."

When I found out I was pregnant, I hadn't thought far enough ahead to determine whether Blaine and I would find out the sex of our baby before it was born. Would we do one of those gender reveal parties or just keep it a secret between the two of us? A secret that only we shared until the day our little bundle of joy was born. I had so much hope until I didn't. I stared out the window.

"Are you okay, Sadie?"

I nodded. "Oh, I'll be fine. I just wonder if I'll ever see my friends and family again, you know?"

"You've never talked about them."

"I guess I thought if I talked about it, it made the situation too real."

"You're married?"

"Yes."

"Any kids?"

Without thinking, I put my hand to my belly and quickly moved it away after realizing what I had done. "Not yet. But it's what I've always wanted. We tried for years — it wasn't easy for us."

It would all have been worth it if I could hold my baby in my arms.

"No?"

"No. We did IVF for a while, but it took too much of an emotional toll on my marriage and me. We finally took a break from all of it."

"Things were good at home?" she asked, as if she knew they hadn't been.

"No, but I hoped things would get better. Now I don't know if I'll ever see him again."

"You think there's a way to get out of this?"

"I don't know. I've failed to think of a plan."

"You see anything when they let you out?"

"There's ocean, and there's the sky. The only obvious escape is to jump off the boat and that would be suicide." I sat on the bench next to Janine.

She cried out in pain and gripped her belly.

Concern flooded me. "Are you okay?"

"Maybe. I think it was a contraction."

"Is that the first one you've had today?"

"It is."

"Just breathe. You'll be okay. It doesn't necessarily mean that the babies are coming right now." What would happen if they were? Who would deliver the babies? What if she needed a c-section? "Just breathe. We'll get through this."

As I said the words, I wasn't sure I believed them.

17

MARTINA

Sipping my coffee, I leaned back in my chair, looking out at the Cold Case Squad Room. People were busy on their computers, some up at the whiteboards plotting away. As opposed to me, who was taking a much needed break. Considering we had little to go on in Sadie's case, I wasn't feeling very confident about what the outcome would be.

My mind was going a mile a minute as I contemplated that there was a criminal couple abducting pregnant women. Were they still at work? Or had they met their quota? My gut said they were likely still a danger to society.

It was definitely time for more caffeine. Putting the thought out of my mind, a new swirl of memories swept my attention back to Friday night. Zoey, Kim, and I had gone out to dinner after we picked up Zoey's flower girl dress at the bridal boutique. Zoey was radiant in her pink dress that looked like a miniature version of the bridesmaid's dresses. Kim had the great idea of adding some additional sparkly applique to Zoey's dress to make her look a little different, since she was the only flower girl. Basically, Kim blinged out Zoey's dress, and Zoey loved it.

Over dinner, Kim helped me talk to Zoey about the idea of

me going on a date. *A date.* I did not know how my girl would respond, and I couldn't believe how she had. Sometimes, I wondered where Zoey got her intellect and keen sense of what was really going on in the world. I had said to her, "Zoey, there's something I want to talk to you about."

She had placed her napkin in her lap and then said, "What is it, Mother dear?"

In my line of work, I had come face-to-face with killers, rapists, and the worst of the worst, but this conversation terrified me. "I was talking to Kim, and we got to talking about a friend of hers from college. A man. She thought maybe I should go on a date with him. How do you feel about me going on a date?"

Zoey cocked her head and made a silly face. "Cool. It's about time."

My ten-year-old daughter had rendered me speechless. "So, you're okay with Mommy going out a date with a new friend?"

"Of course. And maybe, just maybe, you'll get married again like Uncle August and Auntie Kim," she said with a wide smile.

I glanced over at Kim, and she smiled knowingly. Was I the only one who had thought Zoey might have an issue with me dating? She had been so young when her father died, and I didn't want to take any memories of him she may still have. "I don't know about that, but I'm glad you're okay with this."

"Mommy, I just want you to be happy and look how happy Auntie Kim and Uncle August are. Imagine if you had something like that."

I nodded, suppressing the tears that were forming in my eyes. How had I been so blessed with such a lovely daughter? She was loving, sweet, and sparkly. She was my angel.

After that, the topic returned to all things related to Hirsch and Kim's wedding. I wasn't sure how I would feel after the conversation with Zoey, but I felt lighter. Without any more excuses, to date or not to date was all my decision. If I was ready to date, I had the full support of everyone around me. And Zoey was all for it. Feeling confident about my decision, at the end of the night, I told Kim she could give Dave my phone number. That was half the battle, right?

Vincent and Hirsch approached me. "Hey, guys, what's up?"

Hirsch said, "We have some news."

"What is it?"

Vincent said, "We caught Blaine in a lie."

"About what?"

"Blaine wasn't registered for any medical conferences in Washington state or any state for that matter. Wherever he was traveling to, it wasn't to a medical conference."

"What else do you think he's lying about?"

Hirsch said, "Exactly."

There was something fishy about Blaine Jarreau, but I wasn't sure what it was, yet. None of his emotions and actions seemed consistent, one way or another, guilty or innocent.

"Do we know where he was flying to?"

"We can't get airline manifests without a warrant."

"There is no way to get that information?" I asked, hoping not to cross the line. As a private investigator, not contracted with CoCo County Sheriff's Department, we took back channels all the time. We didn't have warrants or law enforcement behind us, and we could sidestep the red tape. But then again, in the private sector, we weren't trying to prosecute in a court of law either. We were just trying to find the truth.

Hirsch said, "Nope."

"Well, if what he told us was true about having his medical practice open Tuesday through Thursday, he'll be back in the office on Tuesday, and we can ask him about it."

"Maybe. Maybe it's better to not let him know we've caught him in a lie just yet."

"Any word from the sheriff about initiating a statewide task force to find out what's happening to all these young, pregnant women and to stop whoever's taking them? If my gut is right, they haven't stopped. It's likely some sort of trafficking ring."

"Not yet. I told Sarge about it, but no word from the sheriff. Without his blessing, our hands are tied."

"But we could reopen Elsa Alvarez's case, right? She was from CoCo County."

"Yes. At the very least, we could try to solve her murder, which then, of course, would lead to the others. But it would just be us investigating, and I think you and I both agree this is much bigger and needs more than two, three, or even nine cold case investigators. This could be huge. I don't think we stand a chance without a task force."

"I agree. Human trafficking is no joke. I know little about baby trafficking, but I'm sure it's lucrative, which means whoever is buying those babies has a lot of money and is also powerful. We will need the support of interagency investigators. And maybe even the Coast Guard."

"Yep, it's big."

Was there really any question whether or not we would open up a statewide task force? Not that I had ever been involved in one, but it seemed like the right thing to do. I guessed, for the time being, we would have to hang back until we received the green light for more resources. Unfortunately, patience wasn't one of my strong suits.

18

MARTINA

HUDDLED IN THE CORNER, I NODDED AS VINCENT GAVE US the latest news. "I called up a few of my friends down south. We have one more woman off the coast of California matching the description of the others. Juanita Velasquez was found dead. She was young and pregnant, with her baby missing. It looks like it all started about a year before Sadie went missing. So, starting six years ago, one pregnant woman went missing every few months down the coast of California. Four dead and then nothing."

"When did they stop?" Hirsch asked.

"They stopped five years ago. A week after Sadie disappeared."

I said, "That's unusual that they would suddenly stop."

Vincent said, "Maybe they didn't. Maybe they found a new way of disposing of the bodies. We should search for missing pregnant women, young or with high-risk lifestyles. I can have the team start right away."

"Good work, Vincent."

Sarge poked his head inside the room. "Hey, the sheriff wants to talk to us."

I glanced at Hirsch. "Let's go."

Hopefully, the sheriff had good news. "Vincent, why don't you come with us?"

Hirsch added, "Yeah, it would be good to have you there. You have all the intel on the women who have been identified so far. We could use you with the sheriff."

Vincent's eyes widened. "Oh, okay."

"It's settled then."

We followed Sarge over to the boss's office. Inside the large room, the sheriff offered us a seat at the conference table. I hoped that was a good indicator that he was in favor of starting up a task force with law enforcement departments throughout California.

We sat across from the sheriff. "I've spoken with your sergeant, and he explained to me you'd like to open up a statewide task force because you think you have found a pattern. A serial killer targeting young pregnant women. Did I get that right?"

Hirsch said, "Yes, sir. Vincent's team has identified four victims in Northern and Southern California and one other woman in the Bay Area who escaped an attempted kidnapping while she was eight months pregnant. She gave us a description of the people who tried to take her. One description matches that of a woman involved in a strange encounter with one of the deceased, described to her mother prior to her abduction. We think it's a couple abducting women and, after birth, killing the women and selling the babies. We have a bad feeling they haven't stopped."

I said, "The pattern now looks like every few months a woman is taken, but the bodies stopped washing up five years ago."

"Any idea why?" Sheriff Lafontaine asked.

"Maybe, afraid of being caught, they found a less visible disposal technique."

"Interesting."

Vincent added, "We plan to search the databases for all missing pregnant women in California, Oregon, and Washington state. All along the coast, we think pregnant women could be at risk."

"That's a lot of speculation. You don't have any evidence the killings are ongoing."

I added, "No, not yet. But it's highly unlikely they've stopped."

Vincent said, "It's true. A friend of mine in the organized crime division at the FBI office in San Francisco said babies fetch quite a lot and unless caught, these criminals won't stop."

Vincent hadn't told us that, but I was happy to hear he had a contact at the local FBI office we could potentially leverage for the task force.

Hirsch said, "Therefore, we think initiating a multi-agency, statewide task force is in the best interest of the public."

"That's a tall ask, Detective. You're talking three different states and multiple jurisdictions. It would be a huge undertaking, and, quite frankly, I'm not sure we have the resources for that."

"But pregnant women are continuing to be targeted. Murdered and their babies stolen. Families destroyed," I exclaimed.

"I understand that. Unfortunately, we can't help everyone. We need to stick with the cases we already have. We just don't have the budget."

My pulse raced as fury filled my being. Was he seriously claiming that he didn't have the resources to stop innocent women and children from being stolen and murdered? I said, "What about Elsa Alvarez? She went missing in our county.

She's one of the victims. Her parents say there was an aggressive white woman asking her a lot of questions before she disappeared. The girl who was almost kidnapped by a couple — a man and a woman — gave the same description of the aggressive woman. They didn't stop. I think they got smarter. We *need* to stop them."

Sheriff Lafontaine crossed his arms over his chest. "Unfortunately, I'm not sure we can do it right now. I mean, maybe talk to the Coast Guard or the feds to see if somebody else can take this on. How about this? Why don't you write up a report, and I'll see what I can do."

Bureaucracy at its finest. Hirsch's expression was emotionless. He always had a better poker face than I did. Vincent looked surprised. Hirsch said, "Sheriff, this is our opportunity to solve a serial killer case. We think that maybe it's even part of something bigger. A trafficking ring. Organized crime. These people don't just stop."

"You're probably right. But unfortunately, we're short on resources as it is. Write me up that report, and I'll see if another agency will take it on."

The room was silent. Filled with disbelief or disappointment? Both?

The sheriff continued, "Well, if there's nothing else, I have a lot to do today. I have a meeting I need to prepare for. Keep up the good work." With that, Sheriff Lafontaine stood up and walked back over to his massive desk.

We quietly left the room and marched down to the Cold Case Squad Room. Once within its walls, I said, "How likely is that report to make it into the hands of someone who can actually give this case the attention it needs?"

Sarge and Hirsch exchanged glances. Sarge said, "Somewhere between zero and half a percent."

Hirsch said, "Yeah, that's what we call a brushoff."

Vincent shook his head. "He's really going to let a set of serial murderers go free? Because of resources?"

Vincent seemed as outraged as I felt.

I said, "It's ridiculous."

Hirsch shook his head. "We can't win them all."

"We can't win them all? Maybe not, but we can at least try, right? Elsa Alvarez is in our jurisdiction. We should see where it leads us."

"If our suspicions are correct, I think it will lead us down a dark and dangerous path. We need more people. Backup. The case is important, but so are our lives. I think we should continue looking for Sadie Jarreau and see where that leads us. In the meantime, pull everything we have on Elsa Alvarez and continue to work that case alongside Sadie's. If it looks like it's bigger than we can handle, we wait until we get backup. The three of us alone can't take on a trafficking ring."

It would've been nice if Hirsch was wrong. But he wasn't. How many other cases were ignored or pushed aside or reports written up when there weren't enough resources to investigate? This was one reason I didn't go into law enforcement and had been a little reluctant to work alongside Hirsch in the beginning. But then we solved our first case together, and I saw the benefits of working with law enforcement as opposed to working in the shadows. Sometimes the truth just wasn't enough. Those responsible needed to be put behind bars so they didn't hurt anybody else. But in this case, we knew there was a big problem, and we couldn't do anything to stop it or to warn the public.

I said, "Whatever," and walked away from the group. I was too furious. Too sad. Too many emotions. Those poor young women and their babies and their families.

Seated, I combed through my emails while practicing my breathing technique. Vincent slid on to the chair next to me. In a low voice, he said, "What if there's something we could do to force them to take action?"

I turned and looked into his eyes. "What do you mean?"

"Well, I think we know from past cases that when the press gets ahold of something, it doesn't get ignored."

I nodded, understanding what Vincent was referring to. If we brought the story to the press, it would make headlines, forcing multiple state agencies to react. And it could warn the public and encourage them to direct any strange encounters to the police. I supposed it could also cause hysteria or panic. The messaging would need to be more proactive so as to not scare. More importantly, the warning could save a young mother from a tragic ending instead of the new life they thought was just beginning.

19

HIRSCH

Bored, staking out Blaine Jarreau's medical practice, I wanted to check in with Martina. She had been more than a little upset by the sheriff's stance on the pregnant woman's case. "You okay?"

She shrugged. "I'm not happy about the approach. It's not fair. And it's terrible. But what can I do?" she said, a bit too calmly for my liking.

"Right. Everything else okay?"

Martina gave me a bit of side eye. "Like?"

I couldn't help but ask about her upcoming date. Kim had told me the guy she knew from college was really nice and was tough, like Martina. Kim and I had gotten into a bit of a discussion about whether it was a good idea to set up Martina. As much as I liked the idea of her finding a partner in life and being happy, I didn't want to push her if she wasn't ready. It was one thing to set up a divorcee, but a widow? I didn't know the rules. But I had assumed that if Martina wanted to date, she'd say so. "Have you heard from Dave yet?"

Martina sighed. "Not yet."

Not exactly a sign she really wanted to go on a date. "How do you feel about going on your first date since Jared died?"

"I think I'm okay with it. And Zoey is more than okay with it. In my life, I've faced much scarier challenges, like serial killers and murderers. How bad could it be?"

"That's one way to look at it. Your date couldn't be worse than a serial killer, unless, in fact, they are a serial killer."

"Thanks, Hirsch. That's all I need to be thinking about — your future wife setting me up with a murderer."

"What can I say? I'm a cop. And I've always thought women should be more careful when meeting a stranger. Not that I doubt Kim's judgment, but you never know. I mean, she ended up with me after all." I chuckled, trying to lighten the mood.

"I'm sure it will be fine. I'm not expecting fireworks or the new Mr. Martina Monroe, but I have been a little curious lately about what it would be like to go on a date. It's been so long since I've dated, I'm not even sure I'll be able to do it right."

"It will be okay, but considering our profession, one tip I would give you is to steer clear of an interrogation. And discussions about morbid topics like murder and autopsies."

"Noted."

Martina flicked my arm. "There he is."

We watched as Blaine approached his midsize SUV and climbed in. I turned on the car and waited. He backed out of his space and headed out of the parking lot. I stepped on the gas and followed behind.

Martina and I had been waiting for this moment for two hours. His receptionist said he normally worked until four, but apparently, he worked a longer shift today. We weren't sure where he was going, but considering he had been untruthful with us, we thought it would be a good idea to follow him around and see where he went and who he talked to. Maybe he lived the life of a hermit and each day was the same. Go to work. Go home. Repeat. But considering he was aiming for a three-day work week, I didn't think so. And I wanted to know how he spent those long four-day weekends.

On the freeway, I waited for him to take his exit home. He passed it. Ah-ha. I gave a quick glance at Martina. She raised her brows. He wasn't going home. Maybe going to the gym. Or did he have a shift at the hospital or plans to see a lover?

After about ten minutes, Blaine took an exit off the freeway and turned down a main road into a residential neighborhood. He didn't seem to know we were following him. A few cars back, we watched as he continued down the street and stopped in front of a light blue house with white trim. I sailed past and made a right turn and parked the car just around the corner. Martina and I quickly exited the car and hurried back to the street to see where he was going.

Crouched down by the blue house's neighbor's hedge, we caught a glimpse of Blaine as he approached the front door. A woman with long, dark hair and matching dark-rimmed glasses stood in the doorway.

Who was she? Had Dr. Jarreau lied to us about having a girlfriend? Blaine entered the home and closed the door behind him. Facing Martina, I said, "We should put our vests on."

"Do you really think he's going to come out with guns blazing?" she asked.

"No, but you never know." Martina had been shot twice since we started working together. And I wouldn't allow for it to happen a third time. It was part of my mission in life to make sure she remained alive and well. Although, both times she'd been shot, she had been wearing a vest, so it wasn't foolproof, but it had saved her life. Obviously, in a bullet-proof vest, you could still get shot in the head or neck or your femoral artery. It was a fact that our job was dangerous, but there was no way I'd allow for Zoey to become an orphan. If that meant I was overly cautious with Martina, so be it.

Before we had time to head back to the car and put on protective gear, the doctor exited the blue house. The woman stood in the doorway and watched him get into his car and drive off. After Blaine was out of sight, she shut the door. "Let's go." And we hurried back to the car, hoping to keep up with him. Breaking into a sprint, we sped out of the neighborhood and headed back to the highway. With luck on our side, I spotted him as he entered the highway.

Adrenaline pumping, I stepped on the gas and raced down the freeway to keep him in my line of sight. At a comfortable distance, a few cars behind him, we took the next exit and followed him through the city streets to Delta hospital, where he worked two nights a week. Following him into the garage, I no longer worried about him spotting us. We pulled into the parking stall next to him. At the end of his car, I called out to him. "Dr. Jarreau."

He stopped and glanced over his shoulder. His face fell. "Detective, what are you doing here?"

"We were in the neighborhood and had a few questions for you."

"I'm so sorry, but I'm very late."

"We'd like to ask you about that conference you attended in Seattle."

He shook his head and pursed his lips. "I'd love to talk about the latest in family medicine, but like I said, I'm in a hurry. My shift starts in five minutes, and I'm running behind schedule. We can make an appointment to talk later." And with that, he ran off.

Martina said, "He seemed freaked out to me."

"I got that vibe too. I sure would like to know who that woman is."

"I'll call Vincent while you drive."

Who was that woman? And why such a brief visit that was seemingly important enough to put Blaine behind schedule for his shift at the hospital?

20

SADIE

STANDING IN FRONT OF THE MIRROR, I TURNED TO THE SIDE and admired my small baby bump. I wasn't sure how closely the crew on the boat were paying attention to my appearance, but if they were observant, they may notice the bump. If I was home, and not being forced to take care of kidnapped pregnant women on some random yacht in the middle of nowhere, I could play it off like I had been overindulging and put on a few pounds. If my calculations from the last time Blaine and I had sex were correct, I was nearing month five in my pregnancy, and I wasn't sure if I'd be able to hide my condition for much longer if they didn't already know.

Although, it wasn't like they were starving us. They made us pretty good meals — the food was nutritious, and they gave us as much as we wanted. The clothes they provided were athleisure wear and easy to hide a few extra pounds. Again, in any other situation, I wouldn't be concerned someone would learn my secret. My mind continued to be boggled by the situation Janine and I were in. We were trapped on a luxury yacht with gourmet meals but couldn't go anywhere or see our families or friends, and in Janine's situation, I didn't think she'd make it out alive.

Janine started having contractions a few weeks back, but they stopped a few hours later. I was relieved knowing it was best for the babies to stay in as long as possible. Earlier in the day, Janine's contractions returned and I was concerned she could go into full labor at any moment. She was only eight months into her pregnancy and I was worried about the babies coming too soon. The babies. Would these people be awful enough to separate twins? What were they doing with the babies? Selling them was the only logical explanation for taking a pregnant woman. They weren't violent with us, other than the guns they stuck in our faces if we tried to ask too many questions or take more freedom than they'd given us.

I glanced out the porthole, wishing I had a clear view instead of the darkened one. As I stared out, I racked by brain trying to figure out a way to escape. Based on what I had seen, the only way to escape was if the boat was docked and then making a run for it. But I did not know when that would happen again. The only time they'd docked since they had taken me aboard was after Rosa went into labor. My heart was heavy for both the baby and Rosa.

I shook all the thoughts away and realized I needed to get smarter. They couldn't take my baby and they couldn't keep me on this boat forever. I wouldn't allow it. Glancing up at the clock, I realized I needed to visit Janine. She had started having regular contractions a few hours before. Last I had checked, they were fifteen minutes apart. At that point, from what I had read, assuming it wasn't Braxton Hicks or false labor again, they could increase in frequency and intensity at any time. The staff didn't seem concerned when I notified them of the condition. The only response I received was the order to monitor her and provide updates if the situation changed.

I exited my state room and walked over to Janine's. Knocking lightly on the door, I said, "Janine, it's me, Sadie."

"Come in," she said faintly.

After I opened the door, I grimaced at the sight.

Janine gripped her belly, her face wincing in pain. I said, "Breathe."

She began breathing heavily out of her mouth in quick successions. The contraction passed, and she peered up at me.

"That looked like a strong one. How far apart are they now?"

"About six minutes."

That was fast. She needed a doctor. "Are they consistent?"

"Pretty much."

Only six minutes apart could easily progress to active labor. The staff needed to know. I went over to the intercom on the wall and pressed the button. "I think Janine is in active labor. The contractions are six minutes apart. We need a doctor."

A static-y voice said, "We'll notify the boss and have her call the doctor."

The boss was a woman? Was it the dark-haired woman? And where was the doctor? On board? I hadn't seen a doctor. As far as I knew, I was the only one to provide medical care to Janine. I'd had to reference the books on pregnancy and delivery when they told me I'd be taking care of her. I hadn't minded the research since I would be in Janine's position before too long.

Janine cried, "I don't want to have my babies here."

I frowned. "I know you don't."

Would they dock for her to have the babies? Would it be our opportunity to escape? Or would she give birth on the boat? It was a large enough yacht, capable of having a room for delivery. It would be strange though, but at this point, I couldn't rule anything out.

Standing next to Janine, I rubbed her back, trying to soothe her. "You're going to have these babies, and they will be healthy and beautiful, and you'll be together." I wished I didn't have to lie about that, but this wasn't the time for hard truths. She needed to focus on delivering the babies and taking care of herself.

The door opened, and one of the staff brought in a bucket of ice chips, cups, and bottles of water. They left without a word. I scooped up a cup of ice chips and brought them to Janine. "It's important to stay hydrated."

She nodded, and I put the cup to her lips. She sucked on the ice. It seemed to calm her.

Focused on the wall clock, I waited for Janine's next contraction. I wasn't sure what to say to comfort her during this time. They had kidnapped her, imprisoned her on a boat, and she was about to give birth for the very first time.

I placed my hand over my belly and prayed to God that this wouldn't be my fate too. Another contraction hit Janine, and she bent over and cried out.

Gritting my teeth, I said, "Just breathe," and guided her in a breathing session until it passed. I glanced back up at the clock. It had only been four minutes since the last contraction.

She was likely near the time that she would need to push. I got up and buzzed the intercom again to provide the update. "Contractions are coming faster and faster. They're only four minutes apart now."

Nobody responded. Frustrated, I paced while monitoring Janine, who had her head bowed. A few minutes later, she was mid-contraction when a member of the crew entered. It was someone I hadn't seen before, but he wore the same uniform as the others. He said, "We aren't able to get ahold of the doctor in time. Sadie, we'll need you to help us with the delivery."

My eyes opened wide. "Right here?" I asked. Me help deliver? I had never delivered a baby before, considering I worked in pediatrics.

"We have a birthing suite. I'll lead you there. The crew is getting it ready now."

That was both good and bad news. "There's nobody else who can help?"

"No. We'll help guide you through it."

Looking at Janine, I tried to hide the fear in my eyes. She looked terrified. She was about to have her babies on this strange boat, delivered by someone who had never done it before.

The man said, "We should go now."

I nodded and took Janine's hand. The man took her other hand and guided her out of the room and down the hallway, which led to another state room.

He opened the door, and another contraction hit Janine. We stopped in the doorway and waited for it to pass.

Janine cried out.

It was a big one. After it passed, we continued inside. I glanced up, and my mouth dropped open. It was a birthing suite equipped with a hospital bed, monitors, supplies, and a baby incubator. We helped Janine onto the bed. "Is there someone who can administer an epidural?" I asked.

"No, we can't get the doctor here in time. I'm sorry."

He's sorry? Trying to push down my rage, I considered if we had everything we needed. I said, "She's having twins. We need another incubator or another place to put the second baby when it comes."

He nodded. "I'll be right back. I'll try to get another staff member to assist and get everything needed to make sure the babies are okay."

He rushed off, leaving Janine and me alone in this bizarro world. Tears streamed down Janine's cheeks. "You're doing great. Janine, you're doing great."

"Have you ever delivered a baby?" she asked.

"No, but it's going to be okay. They have a lot of medical equipment, and they said they'd make sure everyone is healthy." I added that last part. He didn't say everyone, he said to make sure the babies were okay. I held her hand as another contraction hit. My heart was nearly pounding out of my chest. I couldn't believe I was about to deliver a baby. Two babies. I needed to be prepared. It could happen at any moment. Rushing over to a supply cart, I pulled out gloves and a mask. Gloved and masked, I was ready. Well, as ready as I'd ever be.

The staff returned with additional supplies. The woman with the dark hair said, "I'll assist you. Don't worry. We have all the equipment we need to cut the umbilical cords and clean and care for the babies. Everything is going to be fine."

Was it? I said, "I don't know how to check to see how dilated she is."

"The doctor usually does that. But I know what he does." She looked at me and at Janine. "I'll help."

The dark-haired woman put on a pair of gloves and got to work. She turned around and said, "She's ready." She paused and looked over at me. "It'll be okay. I've observed a few times. We can do this. We can. She needs to start pushing. You coach her. I'll collect the babies."

Nodding, I wondered how someone holding others captive could also be kind. I walked over to Janine's side and took her hand in mine. "Janine, it's time. On the next contraction, you need to push."

THE BABIES WERE TUCKED IN BLANKETS LIKE LITTLE burritos while Janine slept peacefully. I wondered if I'd ever get her labor screams out of my head. As she rested in the bed with a baby on either side of her, I wondered what was coming next. How long would they keep Janine and the babies?

The door creaked open, and the crew stiffened. "Ma'am, good to see you."

"Give me the full report."

The voice was familiar. Too familiar. *It couldn't be.* I turned around to look at the woman wearing a blue surgical mask that the crew was taking orders from. As her dark blue eyes met mine, I couldn't believe what I was seeing. Heart thudding in my chest, I asked, "What are you doing here?"

21

MARTINA

On foot, I approached the blue house with white trim and surveyed the area. The property records on the blue house showed it was owned by a Loretta Davidson. But upon contacting Ms. Davidson, she informed us the home was rented to a woman named Jenna Stinson a few months ago. Vincent's team searched records for Jenna Stinson and was more than a little surprised that she had no records. In other words, she didn't exist.

My cover was that I was a neighbor from a few streets over, looking for my lost dog. With a leash clutched in one hand, I strolled up the sidewalk, peering under bushes and down driveways, looking for my fake dog. I wondered who this woman living in the blue house could be and, more importantly, who was she to Blaine Jarreau? Maybe it had nothing to do with Sadie's disappearance or it had everything to do with it. In my experience, a fake ID meant the person was hiding something. What was Blaine doing with someone with a false identity?

We had so very little to go on for what could have happened to Sadie. The woman with a fake identity could mean anything. Maybe Blaine was a drug addict, and the woman was his dealer.

Maybe Sadie found out Blaine was an addict and threatened to leave him and they fought and he killed her. Or had someone killed her? None of it made sense. I wasn't sure Blaine was guilty of killing Sadie, but I was sure he was guilty of something. I could feel it in my bones. His cagey answers. He lied about attending a medical conference. And refused to speak with us before running off to his shift in the hospital, insisting we make an appointment. Alarm bells were ringing. What on earth was Blaine Jarreau up to?

If he was innocent, why would he avoid us? Nothing in Blaine's background came back as suspicious. No criminal records and no apparent financial motive to get rid of Sadie. From all accounts, he was a well-respected physician and wasn't dating anyone and hadn't been having an affair. Although if Sadie had suspected her husband of cheating so much that she had confided in her best friend, he must have been hiding something. If not another woman, then what?

Looking concerned, I passed the blue and white house slowly with Barney's leash in my hand and continued down the block. I had been pacing the neighborhood for at least an hour, hoping to get a glimpse of the woman to find out more about her. Like if she had visitors or if she had somewhere to go. We didn't want to question her cold, knowing nothing about her. My next round down the street, I caught movement at the house, and the garage door opened. It was garbage day, and the woman was bringing out her garbage bins. *Bingo.* As she wheeled out her green bin, I said, "Excuse me, ma'am. I'm looking for my dog. Have you seen him? He's small, about ten pounds. Black and fluffy."

The woman stared at me. "No. Are you from around here?"

She was suspicious of me. That wasn't a normal response. This woman was definitely hiding from someone or something.

"I just moved in a block over. I turned my back for a second to bring out the garbage and he ran off."

"Where are you from?" she asked in an untrusting tone.

"Originally, I'm from Oregon. I'm sorry. I'm so rude. My name is Tina and you are?"

"Jenna."

"It's nice to meet you, Jenna. If you find him, he's wearing a collar. It has my phone number on it. I'd really appreciate it if you called me."

"Of course. Good luck, Tina."

I nodded and continued on my journey. There was something odd about the woman. She was automatically suspicious of me, and people who suspect others typically had something to hide themselves. What was Jenna Stinson hiding? And more pertinent, what was her true identity? I continued on until I could find cover behind a hedge. I watched as Jenna continued putting out her bins. When she finished, she closed the garage door and was out of my line of sight.

I pulled out my cell. "Hey, Hirsch."

"How's it going?"

"I just talked to her. She said her name is Jenna."

"Which we know is a lie. Did you learn anything interesting?"

"Not yet, but it's my favorite day for a stakeout. It's garbage day."

"Jackpot."

"Exactly. I'm going to head back to the car now. See you soon."

Back inside Hirsch's car, I said, "All right, we can come back later to do a little dumpster diving."

"Oh, goody. My favorite."

"Mine too." My first thought was we could come back after nightfall and try to find a piece of trash containing her fingerprints or DNA or some trace evidence within those garbage bins that could point us to the woman's true identity.

"All we need is a set of fingerprints, right?" Hirsch asked.

"Yes. But I wonder if we should stay and keep an eye out. She seems suspicious of me and probably of anybody. What if I spooked her, and she brings the garbage bins back inside?"

"You really think she'd do that?"

I shrugged. "Maybe. I don't think she bought my lost dog story."

"Really?"

"She practically interrogated me, wanting to know where I lived and where I was from."

"Well, we could go back now, and one of us could be the lookout."

Unzipping my backpack, I grabbed my black baseball cap and tugged it on the top of my head. "All right, let's do this."

Hirsch nodded. We quietly exited the car and headed back down Dennis Street. We stood near the driveway and peered over at the house. I said, "The shades are drawn, and I don't see any cameras."

"I don't either. You go ahead and I'll stand watch."

I nodded and tip-toed toward the house while surveying the area, making sure nobody could be watching me. Not that it mattered that much, considering I was technically a civilian, and I was just out looking for my dog. *Kind of.* Actually, I had learned I could get the sheriff's department in trouble if I was caught trespassing since I was contracted and therefore acting on their behalf. But if she caught me going through the garbage, I could run off or say I was tossing some trash in the bin. She didn't know who we were.

All we needed was her identity. The evidence collected didn't need to hold up in court. I casually strolled to the bin and lifted the lid. The trash was in white plastic bags. Not wanting to look suspicious taking out an entire bag of garbage and carrying it through the neighborhood, I opted to look in the recycling bin instead. The woman's recyclable items were also in white plastic bags. *Ugh.* White plastic trash bags are not recyclable. Different fight for another day. Through the bag, I could see cans and bottles. Fingers crossed her fingerprints and DNA were still on them. With no other choice, I grabbed a bag and slowly lowered the lid on the bin and hurried down the street.

Back at the car, Hirsch shook his head as I rounded the car to the trunk. I hadn't planned on grabbing an entire trash bag but considering the time of day, it was that or nothing. Hirsch popped the trunk, and I shoved the bag inside and ripped it open. Cans mixed with banana peels? *Ugh.* I shut the trunk and hopped back into the car. "If nothing else, lock her up for improper recycling. Soda cans and fruit scraps in a white plastic bag."

He smirked. "I'll get right on that."

"Lucky for us, there are soda cans. Let's hope she drank from one of them." Ms. Jenna Stinson's proclivity for Diet Coke may be her downfall.

22

MARTINA

With the trash, namely the Diet Coke can, sent off to the forensic lab to be analyzed for fingerprints, I had done all I could for the Sadie Jarreau investigation. While waiting, I walked over to the whiteboard and wrote everything we knew about the pregnant woman's case.

- Elsa Alvarez from Antioch, body found off the coast of Pacifica.
- Catherine Chester from San Leandro, body found in the Berkeley marina.
- Rosa Ruiz from Bakersfield, body found in the San Francisco Bay.
- Juanita Velasquez from Oakland, body found in Santa Monica.
- Ariana Embree from San Jose, attempted kidnapping.

Even if the sheriff said we couldn't start a statewide task force, we had to find out what happened to the women. At a minimum, we had to solve Elsa Alvarez's murder. Even if we couldn't get everyone responsible behind bars, we could at least try to find the truth. The pregnant woman's case may have nothing to do with Sadie's disappearance, but it was a big enough case that we had to solve it. Too many lives had been destroyed already.

Hirsch said, "What are you thinking?"

"We need to talk to Rosa's family. She's the last one to be taken that we know of."

"Vincent and team are compiling a list of missing pregnant women on the west coast."

"My guess is we'll find more."

"It's sad, but true."

Seriously. How could someone be so greedy and depraved that they would kidnap a young mother-to-be, steal their baby, and then murder them and toss them into the bay? For what? Money — *the root of all evil.*

"I agree. We should go visit Rosa's family and find out everything that happened up until her disappearance. Considering hers is an unsolved cold case too, we can work with Bakersfield PD on it. I'm assuming they'll cooperate."

"I'm sure you can persuade them," I said with a smile.

"I'll do my best."

I sat down and looked at the other two women who had gone missing six months before Elsa Alvarez. Presumably, the first two victims. For a total of four victims and one attempted kidnapping. It was a lot. I couldn't believe we had just stumbled upon it. Why was no one looking for those women's killers?

There had been no news headlines. No proclamation from local law enforcement that they would do everything they could to find out what happened to these women and children. None of that. Not until we found them. We didn't discriminate based on age, race, or gender. We found justice for victims and survivors alike. This was clearly a sign of a serial murderer and most likely some sort of baby trafficking ring.

The sheriff was despicable for not wanting to work with state police to put together a task force to give the case the attention it needed. I hoped that by looking into Elsa Alvarez's case and the others, we could find enough compelling information to bring to the FBI or the state police for them to investigate.

We needed to question all the victims' families, which was going to take some serious time since we would have to travel up and down the coast of California to get witness statements and cooperation from local law enforcement. Maybe Sadie had to wait. "Juanita was from Oakland. We could start with her. She was the first to be found. Once we get some usable information in the investigation, we can reach out to LAPD and hope they'll help on their end."

"Makes sense."

Thankfully, Sarge had sanctioned us to reopen the cold case of Elsa Alvarez. Not that he usually had to give us approval, but considering the sheriff didn't want us to go statewide with this, we'd thought we would ensure we had his backup before proceeding further.

Hirsch said, "I'll call over to Juanita's last known relative."

"Perfect."

Vincent strolled over to the whiteboard. "So, you guys found yourselves another serial killer?"

"Not us. You're the one who found him."

"Four women. How has this not been made public?" He shook his head.

"No kidding."

"Will you talk to the other victims' families?"

"Yep."

"Mind if I tag along?"

"Sure. But you'll have to sit in the back since you are the youngest," I half-teased.

"Don't I know it?"

Hirsch returned. "The phone number is out of order. Vincent, I need information on all known relatives, associates, friends, and boyfriends of Juanita. I want to know everything about her and her world."

"I'm on it, boss." And with that, Vincent hurried out to his tech cave.

Before I could make a comment, Hirsch got another phone call. "Hirsch."

I watched and waited as Hirsch squished up his face and shook his head. "Thanks, Kiki."

Kiki Dobbs was the head of the forensics lab. Fingers crossed she had some good news for us.

Hirsch said, "They got a hit on the fingerprints from the Diet Coke cans."

"And?" Was Hirsch becoming more like Vincent and wanting a dramatic punchline? I didn't know if I could handle two of them.

"It's Breanna Jarreau's fingerprint."

My eyes widened. "Blaine, our missing person's husband, who swears he had nothing to do with his wife's disappearance and says he hasn't spoken to his sister in ten years and doesn't have her contact information... was at her house *two days* ago?"

Hirsch said, "I say we go pay the good doctor a visit."

"Let me get my coat."

"On second thought..."

I stopped. "What?"

"Maybe we put a tail on the doctor and his sister? They're more likely to slip up if they don't think we're on to them."

He had a good point. "True. If we follow them around, who

knows what else we'll find? Considering after only one day, we found out he was lying about being in contact with his sister."

"What else is he lying about?"

Probably a lot. Glancing at the clock on the wall, I said, "I'll call over to his office and see if he's in. We likely have a few hours before he'll head out for the day."

Hirsch said, "We know nothing about Breanna's routine. According to records, she doesn't have a job."

"We can watch the house, but it'll be tough to be in two places at once."

"We'll split up and ask Vincent to help with surveillance."

Excellent plan. What were the Jarreau siblings really up to?

23

___

MARTINA

FROM THE CORNER OF THE PARKING LOT, I SPOTTED BLAINE exiting the medical practice. He casually strolled out and headed straight for his blue Toyota Rav4 without looking over his shoulder or fidgeting with his keys. He entered his car as if he didn't have a care in the world. Hirsch had been correct. It was better that Blaine didn't think we were on to him or had caught him in multiple lies. Knowing he hadn't been truthful could give us leverage later on.

He had no obvious motive to get rid of Sadie, but that didn't mean he hadn't been involved in her disappearance. Maybe she had learned something about his big secret, and he killed her to keep her quiet. It didn't mean Blaine didn't care for Sadie; it meant he didn't love her enough to put her above whatever he was trying to hide.

The sun had already set, and my headlights were less inconspicuous than was ideal for a stakeout. Thankfully, there were enough cars on the road to tuck me behind a few. It was rush hour, and there were streams of cars everywhere, making it a little easier to hide but not to maneuver if he made any sudden movements. After a short while, he exited the highway and headed toward his and Sadie's home. Sure enough, he pulled into the driveway, slowing only to wait for the garage door to open. Blaine moved his vehicle inside, and the garage door descended.

Parked across the street, I turned off my engine and headlights.

The house was dark, but moments later, a light flickered on and another and another. It was likely nobody else was in the house. If there had been, a few lights would've been on. Blaine was alone. The questions were, was he going to stay home and would he stay alone?

Leaning back, I stared at the house, remembering why I couldn't stand stakeouts. They were boring, and I easily tired of sitting for so long. I wanted to find Sadie for the sake of her family, but my mind couldn't stop going back to the pregnant women who'd been killed and had nobody looking for their killers. It had made me think that my time would be better spent searching for leads on the pregnant woman's case than sitting outside the doctor's house. I wished I could tell Hirsch to get some lower-level folks to watch Blaine to free up our time. The problem was we didn't have any. We had our squad, and that was it. We had no newbies to leverage.

An hour later, a few of the lights in the home shut off. Would he be leaving? Someone coming over? Undetermined.

I pulled out my phone and called Hirsch. "Hey."

"What's up?"

"Blaine's at home. No movement from anyone inside or outside the house in the last hour."

"I'm still outside Breanna's. She hasn't gone anywhere either. I'll keep you updated."

"Okay. I'm going to call Vincent and see if he found any information about the first two victims."

"Good idea. Hopefully, we can find them and the contact information for Juanita's family."

"Exactly. Talk to you later." At least I could do some work on the pregnant woman's case while I watched the house.

After dialing Vincent, I said, "Hey, it's Martina."

"What's up?"

"Have you found any more information about Juanita's family yet?"

"Yeah, I got a hit on who I think is maybe her sister. I can give you the details, and you can check it out."

"Thanks."

"I'll send it over."

"Thanks, Vincent."

With my eyes still on the house, I opened my text messages and memorized the number and called Juanita's sister.

"Hello?"

"Is this Marietta?"

"Yes."

"Hi, Marietta. I'm an investigator working with the CoCo County Sheriff's Department in the Cold Case Division. We're looking into a series of disappearances of young pregnant women. We're hoping to talk to you about your sister, Juanita."

"Did you find out who killed her?"

"Not yet. We've just reopened the case. Can I come by and ask you some questions?"

"Yes, of course."

"Are you available this evening?" I asked, hoping not to sound so eager. But I was eager.

"Yes. That would be fine."

After collecting her address, I said, "I'll be there in a few hours," hung up, and redialed. "Hey, Hirsch."

"What's up?"

"Nothing new here. But Vincent found Juanita's sister. I just spoke with her, and I want to go over and interview her tonight. Maybe Vincent can fill in for me here at Blaine's house?"

"Fine by me."

"Anything interesting going on at Breanna's?"

"Nope."

"All right, I'll talk to you later."

I hung up the phone and stared back at the house before dialing Vincent and explaining what I needed from him. Without hesitation, he agreed to take my post.

An hour later, my phone buzzed. "Hey, Vincent."

"I'm just down the block."

"All right, I'll move out so you can move in."

"Thanks. Good luck with Juanita's sister."

With that, I drove off and headed toward Oakland to meet with Marietta. I wanted to know more about these women. At that point, I would have bet my job all the pregnant women's cases were connected.

THE CONCRETE STEPS ECHOED AS I CLIMBED UP TO Marietta's apartment. She lived in a shabbier part of Oakland than I would typically go to at this time of night — or any time of night without backup, but I was armed with a weapon and a purpose. In front of the door, I raised my arm to knock when it opened as if it were magic. Or Juanita's sister had been anxiously waiting for me. On the other side of the door was a woman in her late twenties with chestnut hair and olive skin.

"Marietta?"

"Yes, and are you Martina?"

"Yes."

"Please come in."

She led me into a small dining room. The carpeting was

stained, and from the living room, the TV blasted cartoons. "So, you're trying to look for Juanita's killer?"

"We are."

"It's about time. Are you a cop?"

"No, I'm a contractor with the CoCo County Sheriff's Department. My partner, Detective Hirsch, is usually with me, but he's currently unavailable. And to be frank with you, I don't think this case should wait anymore. Juanita was not the only young pregnant woman found murdered with her baby taken."

Marietta's eyes widened. "She wasn't?"

"No. We've found three others."

"They told us there wasn't enough evidence, and it was too hard to find her — and then they found her body. If they had just looked for her when I reported her missing, maybe she'd still be alive." Bitterness dripped in her voice.

"You were the one to report her missing?"

"Yes, they said she probably just ran away or had a fight with her boyfriend. I knew that wasn't the case."

"Why did you think something was wrong?"

"Because she wasn't with her loser boyfriend anymore. And she wasn't planning to keep the baby. She already had everything worked out."

"What do you mean, everything worked out?"

"She met an adoption agent that matches up pregnant women with potential adoptive parents."

"How did she find the adoption agent?"

"At work. Chance meeting."

"Did she ever meet with the agent outside of her work?"

"She did. It was about two weeks before she disappeared. That's how I knew she didn't run away. Everything was worked out, and she was going to get paid."

"Do you know the name of the adoption agent?"

"I don't know, but I kept all of Juanita's things. Maybe there's something in them. My mom wanted to throw out her stuff, but I couldn't. She's my only sister, and when she died, part of me died too."

"I'm sorry for your loss."

She nodded. "I'll get the box."

Marietta retreated to the hallway, and I spotted a little girl, about three years old, with her finger in her mouth, staring at me inquisitively. I smiled and waved. Her eyes lit up, and she smiled before running back into the living room to watch her cartoons. Marietta returned with a small box. "Is that your daughter?"

"Oh, yeah, that's Gracie. She's very curious and loves cartoons."

"She's adorable."

"Thanks. Here are Juanita's things. I also have a box with all of her clothes and makeup and things like that, but I figured you wouldn't need those."

Maybe. Maybe not. I stood up and opened the box and shuffled through some papers and photos of Juanita with what looked like her friends, her sister, and other family. My heart tugged. A young life snuffed out. For what? Money?

Nothing seemed to point to an adoption agency. I picked up a notebook that looked like a diary. As I flipped through the pages, a business card fell on to the carpet. I picked it up, and I thought, *I'll be darned.* Erica Benton, adoption agent. "I found it."

Marietta looked at the card and nodded.

"Did you ever meet the adoption agent?"

"No, it was just Juanita who went to meet her."

"What about the boyfriend?"

"He didn't go. He was kind of a loser... more than kind of."

"But to give up the baby for adoption, she would need him to sign off."

"Yeah, she knew that, and she talked to him about it. She said he didn't care as long as he got his cut of the money. Like I said, he's a loser."

"Do you know where the meeting with Erica Benton took place?"

"Nearby, at the corner deli. She said the lady was very nice and came all the way to our neighborhood to talk to her. It kills me. She was so happy, and she felt like it had given her a second chance. She wanted to go to college, and she knew she wouldn't be able to if she had to support a baby." Marietta quieted and lowered her head.

"I will find out who killed Juanita and the others. You have my word."

"The police couldn't do it."

I smirked. "I'm not the police."

She nodded.

"Do you mind if I take this card with me, as well as a few of these photos of Juanita?"

"You can take them."

"I will return them after the investigation is done."

"Thank you for not forgetting about Juanita."

"Just doing my job." With that, I exited the apartment quietly.

The truth was, the public had forgotten Juanita. Or was it that they never knew her name to begin with? Juanita's case had been buried and forgotten. She deserved better, and so did those other three women who were killed.

24

SADIE

SHE NARROWED HER EYES. "WE CAN'T GET INTO THAT right now. The number one priority is the babies."

How? What? I mean, I was never her biggest fan. But this? Blaine had said she'd gotten into trouble in her youth, but baby stealing, kidnapping, and murder? How could I not have known that Breanna, my sister-in-law, was capable of such horrific things? I never knew her very well since she and Blaine weren't close. He said she'd been a troubled child and had struggled in her early adulthood with staying on the right side of the law. He had insisted she had gotten better but remained distant from her. Is that why they'd kept me and had not killed me? Because I was the boss's sister-in-law? Had Breanna been using Blaine's boat for her criminal activities? The picture became more clear. Not perfect — it had a few fuzzy spots. But this explained how they knew I was a nurse and why they had kept me alive. Did that mean she would let me go? Would she really kill her own sister-in-law and make her brother a widower?

I hurried over to Breanna's side. "What are you going to do with the babies?"

"That is none of your concern, Sadie. I need you to not ask questions. If you keep your mouth shut, you'll be fine. Okay?"

The pit in my stomach told me this wasn't all going to be okay. However, maybe I could use her words against her. If I made Breanna believe I didn't think they would harm me because of our family connection, it could provide me with the opportunity to escape. But I didn't actually believe for one second I was going to survive this ordeal, especially since I knew her, the mastermind's — the serial killer's — true identity.

Shaking off the thoughts of my impending doom, I hurried over to Janine's side. Her eyelids fluttered. "My babies."

Breanna walked over, holding up the baby boy. "Not to worry, Janine. They're both doing great. But I think this little guy is hungry. We can have you try to feed him, okay?"

Janine nodded and reached her arms out for her baby boy. She stared down at his squishy little face, and tears streamed down her cheeks. "My little man."

"It's important that he feeds," Breanna encouraged.

Janine smiled and pressed the baby to her nipple. She winced, and Breanna assured her, "It may hurt a little at first, but it'll get better."

Janine said, "I read that."

Another baby cried out. It was the girl. I was trying not to get too emotional, but as an expectant mother myself, it was hard not to be. Everything Janine had gone through, I would go through the same thing in a few months. Hopefully, with just one baby. I didn't even know if it was multiples or the sex. I had never had an ultrasound done. All I had was a stick with a plus sign. *Pregnant.*

Breanna picked up the crying baby girl and walked her over to me. "Would you like to hold her?"

I nodded and reached out my arms for the little bundle, and I had to choke back the tears. "She's beautiful."

Breanna said, "She is."

I glanced up at Breanna. "How long will they stay with Janine?"

Breanna's eyes turned dark. "You don't need to concern yourself with those types of matters. The babies will stay with Janine, and you'll help her, and everything will be fine." With that, Breanna turned on her heel and exited the birthing suite.

Only one other member of the crew remained in the corner. Were they there to help? Not likely. They were probably standing guard as usual. I had to admit, my mind was blown.

Breanna was the boss? I could barely process the information. Had I missed all the signs the last time I had seen Breanna? That was Christmas of the previous year, and she didn't seem like a kidnapping, murdering, baby-stealing psycho back then. No, but there was always something kind of off about her. She was awkward and cagey when you asked her anything about her life. Perhaps it was because she was a horrible criminal.

More than ever, I realized how badly I needed to get off this boat. They had to make an exchange at some point. Otherwise, how would they sell the babies? My guess was they would dock to complete the transaction and that would be my chance. If I made it that long.

Was knowing Breanna going to be my undoing? That was what I feared. Not that things were great as it was, but now that I knew the name behind the entire operation, I wouldn't be surprised if I were at the top of the list for elimination.

Janine had stopped nursing the baby and was sitting up, rocking him gently from side to side.

"Would you like to hold your baby girl too?"

She grinned and nodded. She scooted the boy into the crook of her right arm, and I placed the baby girl in her left. "It's a beautiful picture."

"I can't believe they're mine."

"Congratulations, Janine. They are absolutely beautiful."

Without thinking, I once again placed my hand on my belly, and Janine's eyes met mine. Her mouth dropped open. "You're pregnant."

"Yes, but they don't know. I don't want them to know," I said, crying.

"Why not?"

If Janine hadn't figured out what was going on, I didn't want to be the one to tell her. "I don't know, I just don't." If only I hadn't chosen to surprise Blaine. I could have easily made him dinner or breakfast at home, and I would not have been in that situation. I had been too excited and wanted to do something special. Something we would tell our child about when they were older.

Breanna returned to the room, still wearing the mask. "Sadie, we need you to come up to the top deck with us."

"But Janine needs me."

"Edgar will help her. Edgar."

The man in the corner nodded.

Without an actual choice, I knew I had to go with her. My body trembled as I followed Breanna up the stairs to the bow of the boat. A man with a gun in his grip stood waiting. Breanna said, "I'm sorry this had to happen, Sadie. I wish it hadn't. But this is goodbye."

At that moment, I realized I only had one card left to play. "I'm pregnant."

Breanna raised her hand as if to stop the shooter. "You're pregnant?"

I nodded. "Blaine doesn't know. It was why I went to the boat that night — to surprise him with dinner and tell him I was pregnant."

"I don't believe you."

"The pregnancy test was with my things. I had brought it

with me to show him." Realizing it may still be on the boat, I thought maybe it would be a clue for whoever was looking for me. Assuming Breanna and her goons hadn't disposed of my purse.

Breanna shook her head. "Keep an eye on her. I'll be back." Breanna scuffled away.

Across the boat, I could see she was making a phone call. She was the boss, after all. What did that mean for me? Had I saved my life and my baby's? I hoped so, even if only temporarily.

25

HIRSCH

Smiling, I said, "I'm sure whatever you pick will be fine."

"But, August, I want your input."

"All I want to do is marry you, Kim. The details of whether there is silver or gold on the invitations make little difference to me."

"You have no preference of whether we have silver or gold on the invitations?"

"I have no preference."

"What metal do you want for your wedding band?"

I hadn't given it much thought and rarely wore any jewelry. Although when I was picking out Kim's ring, I had chosen a platinum setting for her. "Maybe something that matches your ring. Platinum, silver, or titanium." I recalled the salesperson saying titanium was all the rage, and it was lightweight and inexpensive.

"So you want silver tone?"

"Yes." Nice and definitive.

"Then silver invitations, it is."

"Perfect." At least I got one thing done while sitting here for the last three hours watching Breanna Jarreau's house.

"Should we also have silver tone for the dishes, the place settings, and the wineglasses?"

"I think that would be great." I didn't really know if it would be great or good or that it mattered. But as much as the details didn't matter to me, I knew they mattered to Kim, and she wanted my input. Even if I didn't care, I tried to give it to her. Even though whatever she picked, I would have been fine with.

"You know we have the food tasting on Saturday? And we need to schedule the last fitting for the tuxedos for you and your brother?"

"Yes."

The lights in the house flicked off. "Babe, I'm gonna have to call you back."

"All right, love you."

"Love you, too." I put the phone down and watched as the lights one by one in the home turned off and the garage light turned on. Breanna Jarreau was on the move. The garage door opened, and a silver Mercedes backed out of the driveway. I gave it two paces before I took off in pursuit. The background checks didn't find any employment records for Breanna over the last several years. Yet, she had money to rent a house and drove a luxury car. Something didn't add up. It was nearing eight o'clock at night, and I wondered where she was going. To meet a friend for dinner? Or perhaps an illegal encounter?

Using the car's hands-free device, I said, "Call Martina."

My car said, "Dialing Martina."

"Hirsch, what's up?"

"I'm following Breanna. She just left the house."

"I just left Juanita's sister, Marietta's house. I found some interesting things."

"Like what?"

"Get this. Juanita was looking into having the baby adopted and had met with an adoption agent named Erica Benton."

"We should run the name."

"I've already called Vincent, and he is having his team do their magic."

"At least that's something to go on."

"You want me to join you?" Martina asked.

"I'm fine, but keep your phone on. I'll call if I need backup."

"Okay, but I'm already heading your way."

I hadn't planned to confront anyone, including Breanna, but just in case I had to, it wouldn't be a bad idea for Martina to be close for backup, even though it was late. "Is your mom watching Zoey?"

"Yeah, so don't worry about that. It's the start of a four-day weekend, and she's got her best friend, Kaylee, over watching movies and making art projects."

"All right." I gave her the details of where we were on the highway and which direction we were heading. If I didn't know any better, I'd guess we were going to the far East Bay. Following behind, I thought it might be a long night. "Call Kim."

"Calling Kim."

"Hello."

"Hey, babe, sorry I had to end the call so abruptly."

"No problem. I'm guessing your suspect moved?"

"That's right, and I'm pursuing the suspect right now, but I wanted to call and let you know it may be a few hours. Don't wait up."

"Okay, be safe."

"I love you."

"Love you, too."

I hung up the phone and continue down the dark highway. Thinking back to my conversation with Martina, I was glad she was planning to meet me. I could handle myself, but I had a lot to lose, and backup was never a bad idea.

Thirty minutes later, driving on dark and winding roads, I couldn't figure out where she was going — until I saw the sign. Discovery Bay. Why would she go there? It was mostly a haven for boaters. Boaters. Did Breanna Jarreau have her own boat? If she did, why would she be going out this late at night?

Sure enough, Breanna pulled into the parking lot of the Discovery Bay marina. Stopped on the road, I remained outside the parking lot and waited until she parked, exited her car, and headed toward her destination. After a beat, I parked my car outside the entrance, jogged over to the lot, and knelt behind a fence to call Martina. "I'm at the Discovery Bay marina. Breanna is heading toward the dock."

"I'm only about twenty minutes out."

"Okay."

Phone back in my jacket, I watched as Breanna hurried down the dock until she reached a rather large boat — a mini yacht. For half a second, I thought maybe it was the same boat Blaine used to own, but it was different and was called the *Sea God*. I crouched lower and moved closer to get a better look. Breanna had her phone up to the side of her face. After only twenty seconds, she put the phone back into her purse and waited.

A man wearing a black parka and beanie opened the gate and let her inside. Before shutting it, the man looked both ways. I called Martina back. "She's on the boat. The *Sea God*. A suspicious perp in all black let her in."

"Suspicious?"

"He was looking around like he was afraid someone may be watching."

"Where are you parked?"

"Right outside the parking lot. I'm on foot trying to see what's going on. Dang it."

"What is it?"

"A man in head-to-toe black, a beanie, well-built, is removing the ties from the dock. They're leaving."

"So much for keeping eyes on Breanna Jarreau. We can't exactly see her from shore."

"That was probably by design."

"Does it look romantic in nature?"

"No, not at all. Something is off here. My gut says whatever they're up to is illegal." What was Breanna mixed up in?

"You still want backup?"

"No, I'm going to head back. We can call the Coast Guard tomorrow and ask if they saw anything."

"I'll stay on the line until you're in your car and able to drive away safely."

"I'll be fine."

"What if it was me at the marina?"

Heading back to my car, I said, "Point taken. Let's put in a call to the Coast Guard and have them look into the *Sea God*." I didn't know what was happening on that boat, but I'd bet my badge it wasn't good.

26

MARTINA

I handed Hirsch the coffee with two creams and one sugar. "Happy Friday, partner."

"Happy Friday."

"What time did you finally get home last night?"

"Around eleven. Kim was already asleep. It was the funniest thing. She was in bed surrounded by all the sample wedding invitations she'd ordered."

Smiling, I said, "Wedding planning till you drop."

"Yeah, she's been up to her eyeballs in details."

"Well, it's just a few months away. In a blink, you'll be standing at the end of the aisle watching your bride walk down with her father."

"Two more months."

"Are you getting excited?"

"I am. I just wish Kim wasn't so stressed out. She spends practically every free moment of the day fussing over place settings, invitations, and scheduling cake tastings and food tastings and linens and... you name it. For her sake, I can't wait until it's done."

"You should surprise her with a spa day."

"A what?"

"A spa day. Get her a gift certificate to a local spa so she can get a massage and a mani pedi. Kim would love that."

Kim was one who liked to primp and be pampered. I couldn't imagine spending over five minutes getting dressed, but I knew it took Kim at least an hour with the makeup and the hair and the lord only knows what else.

"You're probably right. That's a good idea."

Hirsch was so sweet with Kim. Not that he was mean to other people, but he doted on her. I was jealous. Not that I wanted Hirsch to dote on me, but it would be nice to be adored by someone someday. Before I could tease Hirsch, my phone buzzed. "Martina Monroe."

"Captain Jack Powder. How are you, ma'am?"

A smile crept onto my face. "I'm doing fine, sir."

"I received your message from last night. And yes, I know, and the DEA knows, all about the *Sea God*."

The DEA? "You do?" I looked over at Hirsch and mouthed Coast Guard.

He nodded, and I ushered Hirsch over to the whiteboard.

Jack said, "The boat is owned by none other than Mexican drug lord Carlos Fuentes."

I wrote the name on the board.

"Never heard of him."

"That's because you work cold cases, and you're not with the DEA. Carlos Fuentes is a known drug dealer."

I wrote *drug dealer* under investigation.

"The DEA's been on him for a while. Anybody who's working with him is no good. How does it connect to your case?"

"Our missing person, Sadie. Her husband's sister, Breanna, was seen boarding the *Sea God* last night after we followed her there. We followed her since we suspect the husband is not telling us everything he knows about Sadie's disappearance."

"Well, now that's a different story."

"What do you mean?"

"I can hook you up with the DEA. They've been watching Fuentes for a while. They suspected he was working with multiple contacts in the Bay Area. Could be that your missing person, Sadie, witnessed a drug deal. Maybe the sister-in-law was using the boat to work with Fuentes and Sadie saw something she shouldn't, and they got rid of her."

"How long has Fuentes been in operation?"

"At least a decade. I can connect you to some folks at the DEA. They'll know more about the case. I'll set up a meet."

"That would be great."

I wrote *DEA meeting* on the board.

Hirsch nodded.

"It sounds like your missing person case is connected to the DEA and the Coast Guard. All the colors of the rainbow."

"That's par for the course around here."

"Is that so?"

"Hirsch and I have investigated everything from serial killers to the mob to senators willing to kill to keep their family secret."

"This is just another day in the life of Ms. Martina Monroe," he said in a flirtatious tone.

"That it is."

"I'll set up the meet with the DEA and call you back."

"I appreciate it Captain Powder."

"Please call me Jack."

"Thank you, Jack."

Hirsch raised his brows.

Yeah, yeah, I suppose I know how to flirt after all.

"It sounds like you made a new friend?"

"Purely professional, Hirsch. Purely professional."

"You know you can bring a date to the wedding, if you'd like."

My cheeks burned as I shook my head. "Let's get back to the case."

"Okay, okay. Based on your notes here, the boat belongs to a drug lord named Carlos Fuentes."

"Yep. Jack said anybody associated with him is no good."

"Like we suspected."

"Jack is setting up a meeting with the DEA for all of us to discuss. But I'm thinking maybe Sadie saw something that got her killed. He said that wouldn't be unusual for Fuentes and his team."

"Maybe the pregnant women's case is a red herring?"

"Possibly." I hesitated, and then I said, "But we still need to find out what happened to those women. They shouldn't be forgotten just because they weren't white."

"I agree, and we'll do everything we can to find out what happened to Elsa Alvarez."

"We need more than to find out who killed Elsa. We need to stop her killers from taking more women."

"I know. But let's take it one step at a time."

As if he could read my mind, Vincent appeared.

"Hey, Vincent."

"Would you like another twist in your case?"

"I sure would."

Vincent was about to say something but paused as he studied the whiteboard. "The DEA is involved now?"

"Looks like it. What have you got?"

"My team ran the name Erica Benton. She has no records. Erica Benton doesn't exist."

It was not that Erica Benton didn't exist. I was certain she existed, but her name wasn't Erica Benton. "Hirsch, what are the odds Erica Benton, also known as an unknown fake adoption agent, is working with Carlos Fuentes?"

"It's as good as any. It wouldn't be the first time a drug trafficker expanded their business to human trafficking. A lot of those people don't care what the product is as long as they're making money. I'm guessing babies are quite valuable on the black market."

The thought sickened me. "I'm so tired of these people."

"I hear you."

"There are so many bad people, and there aren't enough of us to stop them all."

"No. But we can do everything in our power to stop the ones we know about."

But what about the others? The women in a different jurisdiction or other young pregnant women who were in danger. We weren't doing enough to stop these predators. And I found that unacceptable.

27

MARTINA

Outside the station, Vincent jogged toward me. I said, "Good morning."

"Morning. I talked to my guy — it'll go this week."

Nerves coiled around my belly. This was the right decision, wasn't it? It was. If it meant no more young, pregnant women were taken, it was worth it. "Good. I can't stand by and watch another woman abducted and her baby stolen."

Vincent nodded. "The sheriff is nuts for trying to bury this. The public has a right to know. We need to stop these people. You know, it actually surprised me when the sheriff told us we couldn't start a task force."

"Why?" My opinion of Sheriff Lafontaine was so low by that point that I had no expectations.

"Because it will make him look good since we found the pattern, and we'll be the ones to find who is responsible and stop the horror being inflicted on these women. It's a win-win."

"Exactly. The sheriff may not see it that way. Maybe that was how we should have sold it to him. Maybe he would have had another response."

"Maybe. This case makes my stomach turn. You and Hirsch

investigate terrible crimes all the time. Doesn't it ever get to you?"

More than I tried to show. "Oh, it gets to me, Vincent. It never gets easier. You just learn to deal with it better. Like having a reason to live outside of chasing bad guys. Since I've been here, I get to take weekends off — most of the time — to be present with my daughter. And I'm going on a date next week. If you can believe that."

"You're kidding."

"No, I'm not. Kim is setting me up with an old college friend of hers."

"And Zoey is okay with it?"

"She's okay with it. I think more than I am."

"Are you sure you're ready?"

I shrugged. "As ready as I'm going to be."

Vincent was quickly becoming a great friend. It was a little shocking. When I first met him two years ago, I thought he was cocky and young and kind of an idiot. He only had two of those traits. The cockiness was well earned. And he couldn't help being young. He liked to joke around a lot, which could make him seem silly and goofy instead of the intelligent, hard-working, and caring person he was. With Vincent, you definitely couldn't judge a book by its cover. He had such a good heart and always wanted to do what was right.

This wasn't the first time he'd used his media contacts to help other people and get justice for a murdered soldier. A few cases back, a young woman in the Army had been sexually assaulted and murdered. And then it was covered up by the perpetrator and several members of the Army. The perpetrator had been killed by the victim's sister, but all the people who helped cover up the crime within the Army weren't being held accountable. Vincent leaked the story to the press, and it forced the Army to take action against those who had covered up the crimes.

Vincent was willing to stick his neck out on the line and use that power for a second time. I hoped it was as effective as the last time. In my book, Vincent was as solid as they come.

"All right, let's head in."

"How is Amanda?"

He pushed open the doors. "She's doing well. She's really glad we've opened Sadie's case. Her sister May is really grateful, too."

"We will find out what happened to Sadie."

"I believe you will. But who knew the DEA may be involved? Makes you wonder if there's any safe places anymore."

"You can't think like that. The world can be very dark, but you have to remember it is also filled with light and sunshine and puppies and..."

"Rainbows and lollipops and ice cream..." he joked.

"It's true. You have to remember the good things. Otherwise, this job will eat you up." I knew that firsthand. And I'd had more than one person remind me over the years to focus on the good and not the bad. If I only focused on the dark, I didn't think I could get out of bed in the morning and do the job.

The Cold Case Squad room was bustling. Hirsch was already sitting down talking with Detective Wolf. We waved, not wanting to interrupt his conversation.

"What time is the DEA getting here?" Vincent asked.

"They should be here in a few minutes. Why don't you join us?"

"If you're okay with that."

"You brought us the case, and you're helping us with surveillance. This is part of investigative work, too."

A small grin crept onto Vincent's face. "I like it."

"Good. You're good at it and you have good instincts."

Hirsch finished up with Wolf and walked over to us. "Happy Monday. The DEA should be here in about ten minutes. You ready?"

I said, "Of course. Vincent will join us."

"Perfect. We could definitely use your insight and your boots on the ground, if you're up for it."

"I'm up for it, boss," he said with a cocky smile.

"All right, I'm going to grab another coffee. I'll meet you in conference room two?"

"See you there."

Hirsch hurried off.

"I'll call my guy."

"Thank you, Vincent."

Fingers crossed that our secret plan worked.

SITTING ACROSS FROM THE TWO DEA AGENTS, SPECTOR and Florence, I could barely believe what I was hearing. "You've had a team on Carlos Fuentes for nearly a decade, but you haven't had enough to arrest him?"

"No. We've nabbed a few of his lower-level members, but he's hard to get to. We have focused our latest operation on the *Sea God*. It's been under surveillance for the last year. It was previously docked at the Port of Los Angeles. The *Sea God* is registered to Fuentes, and we have surveillance footage with him on it, so if we can confirm the yacht is being used for illegal activity, it should be enough to get him behind bars in the U.S."

"Any idea how Breanna Jarreau is connected?" Hirsch asked.

"We don't know her. At least not by name. We've had one woman coming and going." The agent flipped open his portfolio and pulled out several photographs. "Do you know this woman?"

I said, "That's Breanna Jarreau."

"All right. Finally, a name to the face. They have been working together for a while. We've seen her in Mexico too."

I let that sink in. "How long is a while?"

"She's been in and out of the scene for a few years. We don't know what her role is, but she's definitely high up with Fuentes and his crew."

"How is she connected to your case?" Agent Florence asked.

"Sadie Jarreau is our missing person. Her husband is Breanna's brother, Blaine Jarreau, MD. Have you seen Breanna with a partner?"

"You think the brother is involved?"

"We've caught him in some lies, like the fact that he's in contact with Breanna. Plus a few other small, white lies he told us since we reopened the case." I pulled out the photograph of Blaine and showed it to the DEA agents. "Have you seen him?"

Agent Spector said, "No, I don't think so." He passed the photograph to his partner.

He shook his head. "Haven't seen him."

"Is she usually alone?"

"Yes, or with some guards. The guards are pretty easy to spot. What's Breanna's story anyhow?"

"Rap sheet as long as my arm. Fraud, assault, embezzlement. A real black sheep in her family — comes from money. One brother is a doctor, the other is in banking, and the parents are lawyers."

"I guess all the privilege wasn't enough for Miss Jarreau?"

"I guess not."

"But why did the brother lie about being in contact with her, and how did you find out?"

"We followed him to Breanna's house. She is going under the name Jenna Stinson."

"That's the name we got off the car. She, or rather Jenna

Stinson, didn't have a record, so we've just been keeping tabs on her."

"How do we continue without stepping on your toes?" Hirsch asked.

"It would be best if you stayed away from the marina. You can connect with us and the Coast Guard, but we don't want anything spooking the *Sea God*. We feel like we're close."

"Jack Powder said you thought there might be other boats connected to the Carlos Fuentes operation in different ports in the Bay Area. Like maybe one in Alameda?"

"It's possible. We'll have to check our records. Why?"

"Our missing person, Sadie Jarreau, was last seen at the Alameda marina getting onto her husband's boat. He sold the boat a few months after she went missing."

"Well, if Fuentes had a crew there, it's very possible she saw something that Fuentes's team was up to, and they took her out. Anything that threatens their operation gets eliminated immediately. These are very dangerous people. We'd like you to hold back on Breanna Jarreau until you hear from us and stay away from the marinas. We'll work together on this. Since we are already heavy into it, we need to take the lead. It could jeopardize the operation if you step in now."

Hirsch said, "Understood."

I added, "One more thing. We're also investigating a series of murdered women who washed ashore. All four had just given birth, and the babies weren't found. Any chance Fuentes could be connected to a baby selling operation?"

Agent Spector said, "We haven't gotten a whiff of any baby trafficking, but that doesn't mean he isn't doing it."

"We'd like to keep investigating."

"It should be fine. If you find any link with Fuentes, let us know. He isn't known for human trafficking. He likes his drugs, but in the off chance there's a connection, we'd like to know."

"Excellent. Thank you."

We wrapped up the meeting with business card exchanges and agreement to stay in touch. With the DEA gone, we headed back to the squad room.

Inside our walls, something dark stirred inside me. Yes, we had more hands on the case, but if what the DEA agent said was true and Sadie had seen something she shouldn't, we may never find her remains. And sometimes not knowing was worse than knowing. I wanted to bring Sadie home and those responsible for her disappearance brought to justice. But the faith that we would do just that was crumbling. The DEA had one job — to strike down Carlos Fuentes. Sadie was just an afterthought to them.

28

SADIE

BREANNA RETURNED A FEW MINUTES LATER, WHERE I stood frozen at gunpoint. "You'll continue to help Janine and her babies until it's time to send them home," she spat.

"Home?"

"I said don't ask questions."

I remained silent.

Breanna tipped her head. "Now go to Janine and the babies. Make sure they are thriving. I'll come see you in a few days to confirm your pregnancy." And Breanna hurried off toward the galley.

The man with the gun said, "Go on."

Stunned at the turn of events, I jogged down the stairs and down the hall back to Janine and the babies. That horrible guard was still there, standing in the same corner. I approached Janine. "How are you doing?"

"I'm fine. Is everything okay?"

Shrugging off the sinking feeling in my gut, I said, "Everything is fine. Are you hungry? Can I get you anything?"

"I am hungry."

"What do you feel like?"

"Steak and lobster," she said with amusement.

They fed us well, but we weren't exactly dining on lobster. I supposed it was good that her spirits were up. "How about a sandwich? Or chicken breast and veggies? Maybe fruit?"

"Sandwich and fruit. And those yummy BBQ chips."

"You got it. I'll let them know." I stared at the babies before walking over to the guard. "She needs to eat."

"Use the intercom."

Okay. This whole situation was so messed up. Retreating to the intercom, I pressed the button.

"Yes?"

"Janine needs a sandwich, barbecue chips, and fruit. Milk, if you have it."

"We'll bring it right down."

If they were selling the babies, it was a surprise they would be so concerned with keeping Janine healthy. On second thought, it was probably so she had high-quality breast milk.

How long would they keep her? I didn't think they had kept Rosa long after she gave birth. My estimate was about three days after Rosa went into labor, she was gone forever. Would I be saying goodbye to Janine and those angelic little faces in only three days? Maybe they would stay longer since they were smaller and needed more TLC.

I sat next to the hospital bed while Janine stared at her babies lovingly. She probably never considered that when she finally gave birth to her children she would be out at sea, trapped on a yacht with strangers. Putting myself in her shoes, I realized that was likely exactly what was going to happen to me, except one person on the boat was not a stranger. Would Breanna sell her own niece or nephew? What had happened to Breanna that she had become this — this monster who had no value for human life unless it put money into her bank account? Had she been born bad?

THREE DAYS LATER, I WAS AWAKENED EARLY IN THE morning with a heavy bump. Heart racing, I realized we were docked. This was my chance to escape. I looked out the window, but it was too dark to see anything clearly, but I could tell it was early morning. I crept out of my room, quietly closing the door behind me. The sound of a baby crying kept me in place.

The door to Janine's suite was open. At the sounds of footsteps approaching, I tiptoed back into my room. Keeping the door slightly ajar. I peeked out. Breanna charged ahead while two armed men held the babies.

They were selling the babies.

Where was Janine? I crept down the hall in my pajamas and socks, trying to get a better look at what was going on.

Once Breanna and the gang were up above and out of sight, I tiptoed to the top of the stairs, being careful not to be seen. The sound of shuffling feet and the baby's cries grew more faint. Before long, I couldn't hear them at all.

They were gone.

I poked my head up to take a better look. On the dock, a man stood at the corner guarding the entrance and exit to the boat. Footfall was heading my direction. Quickly, I hurried back downstairs and went into my room, closing the door. The engine roared, and within minutes, we were moving. My chance for escape was gone. I glanced up at the clock. We had been docked for less than ten minutes. It wasn't a lot of time to plan an escape, but it might be just enough for the next time. It would be useful to get ahold of a weapon. Perhaps I'd have to make one. Someone approached my door and then knocked. I hurried into my bed and called out, "Come in." Hopefully, they would believe I had been in bed the whole time.

"Sadie, are you awake?" Breanna asked.

I yawned. "I am now."

"I'm ready to do your sonogram. Please come with me."

Despite the situation, I was excited to see my baby for the first time. I didn't know my fate yet, but I knew I wanted to see my baby's face before I died. Or at least its form in a sonogram picture. I hurried with Breanna down the hall. She led me into the birthing suite that was rather clean and had no trace of Janine. My stomach churned. I wanted to ask where she was, but I knew better.

"Get on the bed."

Without a word, I climbed up and lay back. Breanna was soon joined by the dark-haired woman. "Thanks, Marta. We need to check the status of her abdomen. She claims she is pregnant."

Marta, the dark-haired woman, nodded obediently. She pulled out the paddle. "Please lift your shirt and lower your pajamas, exposing your abdomen."

"Okay." I lifted my shirt and lowered the waistband of my pajamas.

She turned on the machine and then squeezed a blob of gel onto my belly before rubbing it in with the transducer. And then it happened. The thump, thump of my baby's heartbeat. Tears sprang to my eyes. I turned to look at the monitor and smiled as tears streamed down my face. "I can't believe it."

"I can't either," Breanna said rather quickly.

"We tried for so long and we had stopped IVF. I thought for sure I would never be a mother."

The joy was soon replaced by sadness, remembering where I was and that I wasn't likely to know my baby for more than a few days like Janine and Rosa and who knows how many other women that Breanna, my horrible sister-in-law, had killed before me.

Marta said, "Do you want to know the sex of the baby?"

"Yes." I wanted as much of this baby as they'd allow me.

She pointed to the screen. "Looks like a baby boy."

A boy. My son. A mini Blaine. Oh, how happy he would've been in that moment. I was fairly certain he had also given up on the idea of being a parent.

It had been two months since they took me, and I wondered if they were still looking for me, or if the trail had gone cold. Who would possibly know where to find me? From what I could tell, I was at the wrong place at the wrong time.

Breanna said, "Well, I guess you'll be with us awhile longer," and exited without another word.

Marta looked at me. "It'll be okay."

"No, it won't," I said with angry, bitter tears.

She patted my shoulder and then turned off the machine. "You can go back to your room now."

"Can I have a print to take with me?"

Marta nodded. "Sure."

She handed me a paper towel to wipe off my belly. When I was done, she handed me the black-and-white image of my son. Blaine and I had talked about all the things that he wanted to teach a son. Like how to drive the boat, play baseball and soccer, and grill a mean steak. Would Breanna ever confess to her brother she had sold his child and killed his wife? Or would she have a change of heart once her nephew was born?

29

HIRSCH

LISTENING TO THE RADIO, I COULDN'T BELIEVE WHAT I WAS hearing. It was on all the major news outlets. The story's head-line was that a series of young pregnant women had been murdered and the killer never found. They added a note for young pregnant women to avoid adoption agency scams that could lead to their own demise.

Those details could only have come from the Cold Case Squad.

Before losing my temper, I tried to decipher my true feel-ings. Yes, I wanted to make sure other women weren't taken and killed, but this was not how to do that. Yes, our hands were tied by the sheriff, and we couldn't form a statewide task force, but we could investigate on our own. Would it be effective? That was yet to be seen. A leak like this was going to cause quite the storm — one that would strike me and the rest of the squad.

It was my responsibility to ensure my team didn't speak to the press unless they cleared it through our press liaison. Who would do this? I had my suspicions because they had done it before. How was I going to handle it? Or would it get handled for me? This was not good news.

There was a reason they didn't bring me in on it. I was the boss, and they knew I would never allow it. This was going to be a tough conversation with whoever was responsible, and I only hoped the sheriff wouldn't do something drastic in retaliation. I wasn't exactly the biggest fan of Sheriff Lafontaine and didn't always agree with his tactics or his politics or his ways. It was no secret he had tried to use the Cold Case Squad for his own benefit. However, he was our boss. He was the one who approved our funding, and we basically just slapped him in the face. I didn't have proof who was responsible, but I had my gut feelings because I knew my team, and only a few of them would go to this length.

Car parked, I took my time reaching the entrance to the sheriff's department. It would not be one of those days where I reveled in a job well done or the pride in a unified team. I didn't enjoy being a disciplinarian. It didn't suit me, but I couldn't let the whole Cold Case Squad pay for what a few people had done. More importantly, I couldn't let them shut down the Cold Case Squad.

"Good morning, Detective Hirsch."

"Good morning, Gladys."

"The sheriff said he needs to see you immediately."

And the storm warnings were blaring. "Thank you, Gladys." My heart sank. An impromptu meeting with the sheriff was never a good thing. Bypassing the squad room, I made my way to the sheriff's office. I took a deep breath and knocked on the door. Through the glass, I could see the sheriff and Sarge talking. The sheriff walked over and opened the door. "Hey, Hirsch. Come on in."

Sarge shook his head at me.

Sheriff Lafontaine said, "Detective, do you know why we're here today?"

"I have my suspicions."

"Somebody from your department leaked to the press the story about those missing pregnant girls and added the fun fact that the sheriff's department failed to start a statewide task force when they'd learned the enormity of the problem."

Ouch. I hadn't heard that part. "I've seen the news."

"I want names. I won't tolerate this."

Sarge said, "Who was it, Hirsch?"

"I don't have any proof of who did it or planned it."

"But you must have your suspicions," the sheriff said.

Of course, I do. It was my team. "May I ask to handle the situation in my own way?"

"You can ask, but it won't be granted."

The sheriff was obviously beyond names. He was out for blood.

"Look, I won't throw a member of my team under the bus when I'm not sure. I'm sure you can appreciate that, Sheriff."

"If you can't get a name, I'll do it myself."

"I will get the name from my team."

"Detective Hirsch, may I remind you this is the second leak from your squad? The first one I let go because it had nothing to do with me. Or our department. It was the Army's deal, not ours. But now this is throwing eggs at our house. Those responsible will be punished."

"With all due respect, sir, I don't think anyone was trying to bring down the sheriff's department. I think they're trying to bring awareness to other young pregnant women who may be in danger."

"Chain of command, Detective. They undermined my authority. I said no statewide task force. I said you could only investigate those in our jurisdiction. If your team can't toe the line, I think we may need a new team or none at all. Are we clear, Detective?"

"Yes, sir." I knew it was going to be bad, but I hadn't foreseen this.

The sheriff said, "I want a name by the end of the day."

"What will happen to them?"

"I'm still considering the consequences. But what I can tell you is that we will make an example of those responsible. Nobody is getting away with this. Do you understand that, Detective?"

Unfortunately, if my intuition was correct, it was two of our best, and we couldn't afford to lose either one. "I understand."

Sarge said, "Let's go."

I had never seen Sarge so serious. I could only imagine the dressing down the sheriff gave him before I got there.

When one member of the team goes rogue, the boss is responsible. Not that I thought it was Sarge's fault or mine, but perhaps we should have dealt with leaks during the Army case better. We should have explained that it wasn't acceptable then or ever. We marched toward the Cold Case Squad room without a word. Sarge and I were friends, but he was my boss, and he had a boss, so I couldn't fault him for whatever he was going to do next.

Inside the squad room, the team was buzzing until they saw Sarge and me. Vincent looked into my eyes, and I shook my head. Martina's mouth dropped open ever so slightly.

Sarge said quietly, "Is everybody here?"

After scanning the unusually quiet room, I said, "They're all here."

Sarge stood beside the center of the main conference table. "Okay, squad, I need you all to take your seats now. You too, Hirsch."

I complied with the order.

Worried faces filled the room. Sarge said, "You may or may

not be aware, but there was a press leak from this department. You may also not be aware that this team went to Sheriff Lafontaine asking for a statewide task force to work the pregnant women's case and to put out a news bulletin to warn other young pregnant women that they could be in danger. The request was denied. The order was to work on a single case of a missing pregnant woman who later was found dead. Elsa Alvarez. That was the order." He glared down at me. "The details in the news release could only have come from one place and that's this team." Sarge took a breath. "Hirsch and I were just in a meeting with the sheriff. He has given us a clear message to tell all of you that leaks to the press will not be tolerated. Now, I want to know who leaked the case. And I want you to know now that if whoever is responsible doesn't come forward, the entire squad will be suspended."

My heart nearly pounded out of my chest. I glanced over at Martina and Vincent.

Vincent stood up. "Sarge, it was me. I take full responsibility."

"In my office, Vincent. Now. You too, Hirsch."

Martina's eyes were wide. She stood up. "It wasn't just Vincent."

"Oh?" Sarge asked.

"Vincent and I worked on it together. I'm responsible. Vincent was only doing what I asked him to do."

It was just like Martina to fall on her sword. It was noble, but did she know the consequences?

Sarge said, "Martina. Vincent. Hirsch. In my office. Now. The rest of you, get back to work."

Defeated, I looked over at Martina and Vincent, both devastated. I knew they thought what they did was right and what needed to be done, but they had to learn that wasn't how we did things here. There were rules we had to follow. Those rules were there for a reason. And what if... I had to stop myself from thinking of all the terrible scenarios that could happen.

Vincent could lose his job.

We could lose Martina, and I couldn't imagine running the Cold Case Squad without her.

Assembled in Sarge's office, Sarge said, "Shut the door, Hirsch."

The three of us remained standing as Sarge sat down and hit the speakerphone button.

After a few clicks, the speaker sounded. "This is Sheriff Lafontaine."

"It's Sarge. I'm here with Detective Hirsch, Vincent Teller, and Martina Monroe. Martina and Vincent are the ones who put together the press release about the pregnant women."

It wasn't like law enforcement to rat on each other. It wasn't like Vincent and Martina hadn't stood up and admitted what they had done. This didn't feel right. There was something about Sheriff Lafontaine that didn't feel right.

The sheriff said, "Miss Monroe, when is your contract up with the sheriff's department?"

Martina said, "The end of the year, sir."

"Vincent, how long have you been working with the department?"

"Five years, sir."

"Do either of you think leaking valuable information to the press was the right thing to do?"

Neither said a word. But if you asked me what I thought they were thinking, I would say they thought it wasn't that black and white.

The sheriff said, "From your silence, I'll take it you know what you did was wrong. Martina, do you think what you did was wrong?"

"Yes, sir. I take full responsibility, sir."

"Vincent, do you know what you did was wrong?"

"Yes, sir."

"Sarge, take me off speaker."

Sarge picked up the receiver and set it to his ear. He nodded and nodded. "I'm right on it, sir. Yes, very clear. Thank you." He hung up and let out a breath. "I can only imagine the reasons behind what the two of you did. I'm not saying I agree with your approach, but you have to understand that we cannot tolerate leaks to the press from the sheriff's department. Not only have you put your own jobs in jeopardy but the entire Cold Case Squad. Do you realize that?"

They both nodded.

Sarge lowered his head. "Vincent, you're suspended with pay until further notice. Martina, I'll be putting a call in to your firm to discuss the terms of your contract. The sheriff wants us to end it."

Her eyes widened, and I could see tears forming.

I said, "Sarge, that's drastic. I mean, there has to be another way."

He looked at Martina. "I'm going to call Stavros in fifteen minutes. It's been a while since I've looked at the contract, so I'm not sure what the procedure is. For all I know, there is a penalty clause for early cancellation. If it's too steep of a price, we may have to take other action. Do you understand what I'm saying, Martina?"

"Yes, sir."

Sarge shifted his gaze to the papers on his desk. "You're dismissed."

30

HIRSCH

WE EXITED SARGE'S OFFICE, WALKED IN SILENCE DOWN THE hall, and turned right into one of the larger conference rooms. "Martina, you get what he's saying, right?"

Martina said, "I'll call Stavros right away."

Stavros was the owner of Martina's firm, her actual supervisor, and family friend, and I was hoping there was some loophole to keep her contract going. I was fairly certain that was Sarge's hope as well.

"Vincent, I'm sorry. I'll work on trying to get your suspension ended as soon as possible."

Vincent nodded, sadly.

The hard part. I said, "But, both of you, please don't take this as me condoning what the two of you did. I know that you likely had good intentions. But trust me when I say it was lucky Vincent just got a suspension. The sheriff is as mad as I've ever seen him. I feared they would fire you. Not only that, but the sheriff has the power to disband our entire squad. That means he could take away any further good that I know our team is capable of. I want both of you right now to tell me you will never, ever do something like this again."

Martina said, "You have my word, Hirsch."

Vincent said, "It won't happen again."

"Martina, call Stavros. I can't lose both of you." I exited the conference room and headed back to my old cubicle. I couldn't face the Cold Case Squad. *Not yet.* This was my fault. If I let the team know we did not tolerate this, it may not have come to this.

Staring at my old computer and desk, I thought back to my days in Homicide. It was lonely, and there was never a happy ending. I needed to get some air. Hurrying out back, I exited the building and inhaled the frigid morning air. My phone buzzed. I didn't feel like talking to anybody but instinctively looked at my phone anyhow. "Hey, babe."

"What's wrong?" Kim asked.

I explained everything that had gone down that morning. "Oh my gosh, August. I'm so sorry. Can I do anything?"

"No, just hearing your voice makes me feel a little better."

"It'll get better. Don't worry."

"Thanks. I need to get back in there."

"I love you."

"I love you too."

After a few more breaths of the chilly air, I reentered the station as Vincent was on his way out. "We'll be in touch."

With his head hung low, he said, "Got it, boss."

A kick to the chest.

Returning to Sarge's office, I said, "Everything done?"

"I just got off the phone with Stavros, the owner of Martina's firm. He said it will cost us a small fortune to get out of her contract, but he is adding an addendum that states her contract with us is on hold until further notice."

"What does that mean?"

"It means she no longer works here until the sheriff reinstates her."

I nodded.

Sarge said, "Are you okay?"

"This is my fault, Sarge."

"Being the boss isn't easy."

"I know. I'll do better. How are you?" I asked.

"Well, I just fired my girlfriend's daughter, and I'm having dinner with Betty tonight." He paused and said, "This too shall pass."

I waved as I headed toward the squad room to notify the team that two of their own had been suspended until further notice. How would we find out what happened to Sadie without the help of Martina and Vincent? What about the pregnant women's case? This was the biggest blow the Cold Case Squad had ever experienced. It would be a true test of my leadership to keep us going without two of our most valuable members. Shaking my head, I told myself I couldn't dwell on that. I had to be an example.

31

MARTINA

AFTER WIPING MY EYES AND CHEEKS, I STARED INTO MY rearview mirror. My cheeks were still blotchy, but the cold weather could easily explain it. My appearance was acceptable. I climbed out of my car and headed toward my front door. With little energy, I unlocked the door and pushed it open.

Within seconds, Zoey came running down the hall. "Mommy, you're home early." With the events of the morning, I had forgotten it was a holiday weekend and Zoey wasn't in school.

"I am."

"Are you on a break?"

"I'm home for the rest of the day."

"Cool," Zoey exclaimed.

Not cool. I set my backpack down on the floor and closed the door behind me. My mom entered the hallway, looking concerned. "We weren't expecting you home early today, were we?"

"Nope. There has been a change of plans," I said with as cheery of a voice as I could muster.

"How come you're home early?" Zoey asked.

"Oh, it's a long story. We can talk about it later. Let's think of something fun to do today."

Zoey said, "I have just the thing!" and ran off down the hall.

"What happened?"

"They suspended Vincent and me for leaking the story about the pregnant women to the press."

"How did they find out it was you?"

"Vincent was prepared to take the fall, but I couldn't let him take all the blame."

"How long is your suspension?"

"They didn't say. As of right now, I no longer work at the sheriff's department. Hirsch said he would try to get me back in, but the sheriff is behind this, and he wants to make an example of us."

"I'm sure it will all work out. Have faith."

I'll try.

Zoey rushed into the living room with construction paper and a bin filled with tubes of glitter. "Grandma and I have been working on projects of real-life, so I thought maybe we can work on one together." Zoey set down the papers on the coffee table and showed me one. "Grandma draws it, and I fill it with glitter. This one is Barney. I made him blue just for fun. It's real-life but with pizazz."

"I love it."

Barney ran over at the sound of his name. With his tail wagging, I patted his back before scratching behind his ears. "Oh, you're a good boy, Barney."

Barney hopped up on the couch, and I joined him. Zoey moved on to the next complete artwork.

"Tell me about this one."

"It's our favorite park. That's the walking trail where we take Barney and then all the green trees."

"I like all the colors."

Zoey stood up and nodded. "Good. I was thinking we could do one of our backyard. We'll make it look like we're having a barbecue."

Mom said, "I like that. We'll have to do a red-and-white checkered tablecloth. It will add a pop of color."

"Yes!" Zoey exclaimed.

"Sounds great."

"Martina, how would you like an iced tea, lemonade, low sugar?"

"Sounds great." If I wasn't so depressed about being suspended from the sheriff's department, it would be a pleasant day. I supposed it could be, anyway.

Zoey cocked her head. "Are you on vacation?"

"No, just a brief break from work." More like a forced vacation where I would worry every day whether my position with the sheriff's department was over.

My thoughts drifted to the last time I was suspended from work. It was two-and-a-half years ago when I landed in the hospital after a drunk driving accident. Stavros had been furious and told me I was on leave and couldn't come back until I was ninety days sober. Our relationship hadn't been the same after that. It was one reason I took the contract with the CoCo County Sheriff's Department. Stavros and I needed time apart to rebuild our relationship. And I needed to forge a new way for myself without Jared and Stavros always bailing me out when I made poor decisions. I had been sober over two years and thought life was good — healthy. Had I once again jeopardized it all, thinking I knew better? Would Hirsch forgive me? Would it change our relationship like it had Stavros and mine? Stavros and I were in a better place after two years, but it still wasn't quite the same.

I didn't always enjoy following the rules, and that was one reason I'd avoided a career in law enforcement in the first place.

But I really liked my job and the squad and working with Hirsch. I was going to have to turn over a new leaf and follow the rules all the time — not just when it fit what I thought was right. Could I do it?

As if on cue, my phone buzzed. I said, "I need to talk to Uncle August. I'll be right back, okay?"

"Okay."

While lifting myself off the couch, I answered. "Hey, Hirsch."

"How are you doing?"

"I'm all right. I'm home with Mom and Zoey. We're about to do an art project. There's going to be a lot of glitter," I said, trying to keep a lighter tone and not break down.

"That's good. I'm going to try to get you and Vincent back as soon as possible, but I don't think it's going to be easy."

"For what it's worth, Hirsch, I am sorry. I regret moving forward with the plan. I promise you, I won't do anything like that ever again." Suppressing the tears, I moved the phone away from my mouth to do some breathing exercises.

"I appreciate that, Martina. Losing two of my best is not easy. The entire team is down. I need you and Vincent here."

"I'm sorry." I couldn't think of anything else to say. I hated letting him down.

"We shuffled some things around to make sure we can still work our cases. But I just wanted to check on you and make sure you're okay."

Of course. Hirsch had been looking out for me from the moment we agreed to work together. It only made me feel worse. "I'm all right. How are you?"

"I'm fine. A little stressed, but it'll be okay."

We said our goodbyes, and I shook my head as tears escaped. After wiping them away, I returned to the living room. Disappointing my best friend was almost worse than getting

Vincent suspended. Or maybe it was the same. Vincent would not have been suspended if it weren't for me. I should not have encouraged him to go through with the plan. I needed to get it together.

I said, "Wow. The backyard sketch looks great." Mom was an excellent artist.

Mom added, "Your tea is on the coffee table."

"Thanks."

Zoey said, "Doesn't it look wonderful? I was thinking we could use gold glitter for the grass."

"We don't want to use green?" I asked.

"That's so boring, Mom."

"Mom?" What happened to Mommy?

Zoey must have sensed the surprise. "Is it okay if I call you Mom? I'm getting older now, and that's what you call your mom."

Zoey's getting older. A roundhouse to the chest. "It's okay."

"Great!"

A few hours later, we had an extremely colorful glitter depiction of our backyard.

My phone buzzed, but I didn't recognize the number. "I need to take this."

Mom said, "It's time for lunch, anyway."

In the hall, I said, "This is Martina Monroe."

"Hi, Martina. This is Jack Powder from the Coast Guard."

I wasn't sure of the protocol of receiving sheriff's department information. When Stavros had suspended me, he made me return all my work electronics, and I was told to direct all the company business to the office. "Hi, Jack, how are you?"

"I'm doing all right. I saw the news report. It's all anyone is talking about around the water cooler."

"I can imagine."

"Not just the water cooler. We got a call earlier that I think you and Hirsch may want to check out."

"Oh?"

"We received a call from the mother of a missing pregnant woman. It was about six years ago. She said somebody had tried to buy her daughter's baby, but the girl had backed out. And then she was never seen again."

"It could be connected."

"I didn't have a lot of time to talk to her, but she provided her contact information. I told her I would pass it along to the investigators."

"Thanks, Jack."

He gave me the details, and I thanked him and hung up the phone. It was a solid lead, and normally, I would drop everything and call this woman to make an appointment to interview her about her daughter, but it would be a sneaky thing to do behind Hirsch's back. I couldn't do it — I had to do the right thing. The right thing for Hirsch and the right thing for the investigation. I pressed the buttons and waited.

"Hey, Martina, what's up?"

"I just got a call from the Coast Guard. He gave me a tip." I explained the information and provided the contact details for the mother of the missing pregnant woman.

"We'll take care of it, Martina. Thanks."

"Sure." I hung up, defeated.

What now? More glitter? Or go back to the firm and pick up some work while I was on suspension? My gut stirred. If I did, would it be permanent? The contract with the sheriff's department wasn't forever, and I had assumed I'd go back to the firm, eventually. *But not yet.* Sometimes doing the right thing didn't feel right at all.

32

HIRSCH

Sitting across from Mr. and Mrs. Hernandez, I could feel the grief. After they'd explained to me that their daughter had gone missing six years ago, at nineteen, while she was eight months pregnant, I said, "And you don't think she ran away?"

"No, she would not have done that. She was happy about having the baby. At first, she was unsure, especially when she met Erica and Ben and they had offered to adopt her baby."

Erica was the same name of the adoption agent provided by the other family. But who was Ben? Was he the other half of the couple? "Can you tell me how Daisy met Erica and Ben?"

Mrs. Hernandez nodded. "Daisy told me they were customers at the restaurant where she worked. The woman was there having lunch with her husband, Ben, and they asked her about the baby. After she told them she was thinking about putting the baby up for adoption, the man was very interested. He said they were having a difficult time conceiving. They'd tried for years and couldn't get pregnant and were looking at adopting a child. Daisy said they seemed really nice."

"What was the couple's last name?"

"'They introduced themselves as Erica and Ben Benton. When Daisy asked what they did for a living, Erica said she was just starting out as an adoption agent and Ben was a doctor."

"Did they agree right then and there, at the restaurant, to adopt the baby?"

"No. The woman gave Daisy her business card, and they set up a meeting to talk about the terms of the adoption. They said they would pay all of Daisy's medical bills plus five thousand dollars. I told her I didn't like the sound of it. It didn't seem right to sell your baby. It was one thing to go through a regular adoption agency, but this seemed... it seemed off to me. Too good to be true."

"Did she meet with them again?"

"She did, but I told her I had to go with her. I didn't believe their offer was legit."

"You met Erica and Ben Benton?"

"Yes."

"What can you tell me about the meeting?"

"We talked about terms, and Daisy was right. They seemed really nice, but something was off about them. I could feel it. They said they were married, but I had the feeling they weren't, or at least not as happily married as they said."

"Why is that?"

"Well, they kept saying they were so in love and wanted to add to their family, but they never touched or held hands or kissed or anything. They weren't even sitting that close to each other."

"What happened next?"

"Daisy and I told them we would think about the terms and weren't ready to sign any papers yet. After the meeting, we went home and had a long discussion. I told Daisy she should walk away from the deal and go to a regular agency."

Women's intuition? "What did Daisy do next?"

"She was stubborn. She said it was her baby and her decision. She said either way, the baby would go to a good home, but with the Bentons, she'd also get five thousand dollars. She met with them again and signed the papers."

"But you said she changed her mind?"

"Yes, a couple of weeks before she was due, she had some cramping, so I took her to the hospital. They did an ultrasound, and that's when she saw him for the first time. She broke into tears and said she couldn't give away her baby boy. She decided she wanted to raise him."

"She went back to Erica and Ben Benton and told them she changed her mind?"

"That's right."

"How long after she told the Bentons she wasn't giving up the baby did Daisy go missing?"

"It was a week later. She had gone to work in the morning, but she didn't come home, and then I found out from the restaurant she never showed up for her shift."

"Do you remember what Erica and Ben Benton looked like?"

"I do. They were white. The doctor had dark hair, dark eyes, a kind smile. The woman had sharp features with light brown hair and blue eyes. Both tall, thin."

"If you saw photographs, do you think you could recognize them?"

"It's been a while, but I think so."

Our first big break. "Could you come down to the station and look at some photos?"

"Sure. Do you think Daisy's disappearance is connected to the case that was on the news?"

"Yes, I do." I wished Martina was there. Although I didn't agree with her tactics to make the news public, her and Vincent's stunt may have broken the case wide open.

"When do you want us to come down?" Mrs. Hernandez asked.

"As soon as you can."

"We're available now."

"Great." After providing the details to the CoCo County Sheriff's Department, I headed back to my car, wanting so badly to call Martina to tell her the latest on the case. But I thought better of it. She was on suspension, and I did not need to get the Cold Case Squad into bigger trouble than it already was.

33

HIRSCH

STANDING IN THE DOORWAY OF SARGE'S OFFICE, I explained to him that Daisy Hernandez's mother and father were coming in to look at a photo lineup to identify the man and woman who tried to purchase their missing daughter's baby. Sarge scratched the back of his head. "This missing person isn't from CoCo County?"

"No, they're next door in Alameda County, but they gave the same name as Juanita's family. Erica Benton, adoption agent. There's a connection."

Sarge said, "What a day."

"Yes, and it's not over yet."

"This new lead is from the press leak?" Sarge asked.

Sarge hadn't gotten to his position by being dumb. Maybe like me, he was hoping this connection, and bringing more victims to light, would prove that although a leak to the press wasn't the right thing to do, it had helped the case and could end up making the CoCo County Sheriff Department look good. "Yes. We could be on to something huge here, Sarge."

"I don't deny that."

"We need our people back."

"It hasn't even been a day, Hirsch. There's no way the sheriff will let them come back yet."

"We need more people. This is about to blow up."

"Go meet with your witnesses. Let me try to figure something out."

"Thanks, Sarge." I hurried to reception knowing the Hernandezes were right behind me when I left their home. They probably followed all the traffic laws and didn't speed like I had so I could have time to talk to Sarge first. Sure enough, standing close together were Mr. And Mrs. Hernandez. "Thank you again for coming down. Let me take you back to our Cold Case Squad room. We rarely let civilians in, but we have some photographs in there that I'd like you to look at."

If my hunch was correct, we would have the true identities of Erica and Ben Benton in no time at all.

"Okay."

As we walked, I talked. "Do you need a drink? We have water, coffee, and tea. It's not that great, but it's not that bad either."

"I'm fine, thank you."

"Same here."

Considering the time of day, the squad room should be empty. I opened the door and did a quick survey to make sure there weren't any gruesome pictures up. Upon the all clear, I led them into the room. "Please have a seat."

They sat. Just then, Rodolfo, one of our researchers who worked with Vincent, walked in. Perfect, no need to make the call.

"Oh, sorry, Detective Hirsch. I didn't mean to interrupt."

"No, actually, I could use your help. Do you have a few minutes?"

"Sure. What can I help with?"

I said, "I'll be right with you," to the Hernandezes and met with Rodolfo in the corner. "This is Mr. and Mrs. Hernandez. Their pregnant daughter went missing six years ago. We suspect she had met with the adoption agent, called Erica, prior to her disappearance. Could you please bring in all photographs associated with Sadie Jarreau's case and Elsa Alvarez's case? And throw in a few other male and female photos that look similar to the current suspects. And then put the women in a pile and the men in a pile. Print new pictures if you have to. Any questions?"

"No, but it might take me a little while."

"No worries. What, like ten-fifteen minutes?"

"If that. I'll work quick."

"Perfect. Thank you." I hurried back to Mr. and Mrs. Hernandez.

This was the point when I would have turned to Martina and asked her what her gut was saying. After a single day, I was having trouble not having her by my side to bounce ideas off and asking what that magic gut of hers was saying. We needed to get her reinstated.

"Mr. and Mrs. Hernandez. It'll take a few minutes to get the photographs together. But since I have you here, what else can you tell me about Daisy and the father of the baby?"

We needed to have more information. Just because other missing pregnant women had met with Erica Benton, the supposed adoption agent, it didn't prove she was responsible for their murders or their disappearance.

We needed evidence for that.

And we also had to rule out an abusive relationship and make sure it wasn't just a coincidence that Daisy had met with our suspects. It's a known fact that when women who are victims of domestic violence become pregnant, their abusers often become even more violent and it sometimes leads to a major escalation, such as murder. "He's a kid from the neighborhood. José was not a bad guy. Just young and stupid."

"How was Daisy and his relationship?"

"Normal teenager stuff. They liked to go out and have fun. They would break up and get back together every other day."

"Was there any abuse in the relationship? Did José ever hit Daisy?"

"I don't think so. As her mother, I looked out for signs of that kind of thing."

Daisy's father added, "Me too. I always looked to see if there were any marks on her arms or neck. I never saw any."

"Do you think José could have anything to do with your daughter's disappearance?"

Mrs. Hernandez said, "No. When Daisy told him she was going to keep the baby, he kind of freaked out and they broke up again, but nothing violent."

"How did José freak out?"

"They got into an argument. He said they were too young and that Daisy was trying to ruin his life. They broke up, but then he apologized, and they got back together."

Based on that, I wouldn't one-hundred percent rule him out. "I'd like to have his full name. My team will want to follow up with him."

"Okay." Mrs. Hernandez fished into her purse and pulled out a pen and a small notebook. She scribbled on a page, tore it off, and handed it to me. "That's his mother's number and address. He was still living with her last I heard."

"Thank you. After you filed the original missing persons report, did the investigators have any leads?" I asked while making a mental note to get a copy of the missing person file for Daisy Hernandez. This would have been the moment I would have asked Vincent to get me the file. He would have replied with a witty comment and then assured me he would contact Alameda County right away. Without my two star players, the game was rough.

Mr. Hernandez said, "No. They said she probably ran away."

Unlikely. What woman at eight months pregnant would run away? "How was Daisy planning to raise the baby?" I guessed she had little money since she had been living at home with her parents.

"We told her she could stay home with us, and we would help her raise the baby. We were excited for our first grandchild."

Mr. Hernandez wrapped his arm around his wife as if they knew their daughter was gone and so was their grandchild.

Rodolfo returned with two folders in his hand, one labeled women and one labeled men. *Well done.* "Thank you."

"Sure thing."

He handed me the files, and I opened each one. Two perfect stacks of photos. With my adrenaline pumping, I set up the array of men with dark hair and dark eyes. To the Hernandezes, I said, "If any of the men look like Ben Benton, let me know. Please take your time." And then I set up the next set of five pictures of women with medium to light hair and blue eyes and gave them the same instruction.

The couple studied the photographs.

Mrs. Hernandez narrowed her eyes and picked up a few of the photographs of the women to examine them closer.

I had to admit, the photographs of the five different women looked very similar. There were only a few major differences in appearance, like one had a widow's peak, one had a sharp nose. Mrs. Hernandez picked up one photograph and said, "This is her. This is that woman. Erica Benton. I would recognize those evil eyes anywhere."

Mr. Hernandez nodded. "Yes, that's her." He pointed to one man. "And that's him. The doctor."

Mrs. Hernandez said, "Yes, you're right. That scar on his forehead. I remember that now."

For a moment, it felt like time stood still. "Mr. And Mrs. Hernandez, are you sure?"

Mr. Hernandez said, "Yes."

Mrs. Hernandez said, "Yes."

"Thank you. You've been very helpful."

"Do you know who these people are?" Mrs. Hernandez asked.

"We do."

"Who are they? What did they do to our little girl?"

"We don't know for sure that they did anything to Daisy. However, I can tell you they are persons of interests in another case, and I can't disclose too much right now. But we will keep you informed as the case develops."

Mrs. Hernandez interrupted me. "Do you know where they are? Are they free to hurt other people?"

That was an excellent question. "They're local, and we've been in contact with both of them regarding another case."

"What did they do?"

"Unfortunately, I can't disclose that right now." Partly because it was an active investigation and partly because we weren't exactly sure. "But I appreciate you coming down here. You've been very helpful. I will keep in touch as the investigation develops, okay?"

"Will you find our Daisy?" Mrs. Hernandez asked.

"We'll try."

After escorting them outside of the station, I headed back to Sarge's office. He looked worse for the wear. "Hey, Sarge."

"What's up?"

"Our witnesses just ID'd the suspects who were trying to buy their daughter's baby."

"You've got to be kidding."

"We need Martina and Vincent back."

"I'll talk to the sheriff."

I raked my fingers through my hair and grabbed at the back of my head. This case was getting more complicated, and I needed my team.

34

SADIE

On the top deck, I stared out at the vast ocean, wondering what would happen next. Based on my estimate, I had been on the boat for five months. And I could have the baby any day but most likely in a few weeks, assuming all was well.

Breanna checked me regularly to make sure the baby remained healthy and honestly, they treated me more like a guest than a captive. The situation could be worse. They could starve me or do unspeakable things, but we sailed through the ocean blue, and I dined on healthy food with prenatal vitamins.

One fact that had me on edge was that I knew the identity of the boss, and I could essentially go anywhere I wanted on the boat except when we were docked. It was worrisome. I had never been into true crime or been fascinated with serial killers, but I had watched enough movies to know if the bad guy or gal showed their face, the captive wasn't likely to survive. A few times, I had pleaded with Breanna to let me and the baby go and promised not to say a word to the authorities. Her response had been a blank stare followed by, "Not to worry, Sadie. Everything will be just fine."

How can it be just fine?

The crew hadn't brought on any new passengers or captives in three months. It could only mean one thing. I was next. We had only docked at a few different ports for supplies, or so I believed, since I had heard things being brought onto the boat before we drove off again. Those were the only times I wasn't allowed free range on the boat. That rule made it obvious I would never be set free. Why keep up the charade? Probably so I would stay calm and keep the baby healthy. Stress was bad for the baby.

Footsteps clicked on the boat deck, and I turned to see my enemy approaching. "Hi, Breanna."

"Sadie, how are you feeling?"

"Pretty good." Being out in the open air always lifted my spirits and my energy levels. I walked several hours a day. There wasn't much else to do other than read and watch movies.

"That's good to hear. No contractions?"

"None yet, but I would guess I'm a few weeks away from that."

"True, but it could happen at any time. We want to make sure that everything goes smoothly."

"I appreciate that."

She studied my face, as if trying to read me. "We'll be going ashore early tomorrow to pick up supplies. Do you have any special requests? Would you like some new books or DVDs or any foods that you're craving?"

If I couldn't see Breanna's face, I would assume she was being kind. But her eyes were soulless and her body without emotional tells. Was she taking orders from somebody else? Someone who wanted to make sure I was comfortable in my final weeks? But who? Breanna never let on that anybody else was part of the organization other than her crew that had dwindled down to one guard and Marta, the all-around go-getter who also carried a gun and doubled as a bodyguard.

"I would appreciate a few more books to read."

"Consider it done."

"Thank you." I tried to appear cheerful, as if I didn't resent this monster of a human being who'd been stealing babies and murdering women and would do the same to me. I wasn't sure of my plan yet, but I knew that making her believe I wasn't resentful would benefit me. No matter what happened, she didn't need to know the seething hatred I had for her.

Breanna turned to leave but paused and looked over her shoulder back at me. "One more thing. Tomorrow, we'll do another sonogram to see how the little guy is doing. Also, you will meet the doctor who will deliver your baby."

"That sounds nice. What's his name? The doctor, I mean."

"All in due time, Sadie." And with that, she headed toward the bow of the boat, entering the cabin out of sight.

Was the doctor the real mastermind behind all of this? Was he giving Breanna the order to treat me nicely? Come to think of it, of all the action-packed films I'd seen, the hostages were provided minimal food and kept in dark and dirty rooms. It was unlike my yacht captivity. I might have been wrong all along. Maybe they hadn't killed Janine or Rosa. Maybe they hadn't stolen their babies. I knew nothing for sure anymore. I'd like to think that maybe there was some logical explanation. Or it was just wishful thinking and hoping I didn't share their fate. I stared down at my swollen belly and smiled as the outline of my son's foot kicked my belly. He was a strong one. I needed to be just as strong to make sure we both survived.

I made my way to the galley. "Hi, Marta."

"What can I get you?" Marta asked.

She had always been kind but not very chatty. "I'd like a turkey sandwich and an apple."

"Of course. Would you like it out on the deck or brought to your room?"

"In my room, please."

"No problem. Just give me a few minutes."

"Thank you." I descended the stairs and reentered my state room. I would've been happy to make my own sandwich and prepare my own food, but they wouldn't let me. *Smart.* There were knives and other possible weapons in the kitchen I could use to escape.

After my afternoon snack, I lay down and pulled a novel from the shelf.

In what seemed like a blink of an eye, I woke up, and it was the next morning. I scooted out of bed and looked out the porthole. It was dark. The clock on the wall showed early morning, which meant I needed to stay down here since we were docked.

My stomach growled, and I went over the intercom and ordered breakfast before sitting back down on the bench. *Today, I will meet the doctor.* What would he be like? Would he be nice like Marta or heartless like Breanna?

After scrambled eggs with broccoli and cheese, I picked up my book and read as I waited. Before too long, a knock at my door sounded. "Come in."

Breanna appeared. "Are you ready for your sonogram?"

I nodded and set down my book before waddling out of my room toward the birthing suite. "Is the doctor here yet?"

"He is."

"Good." Considering I was eight months pregnant and had never seen an actual doctor for the pregnancy, I thought it was about time.

My healthcare on board had been limited to Breanna, Marta, my nursing knowledge, and the books I read. Marta must have some medical training, since she was the one who had taken blood and urine samples, but I had never actually seen a doctor.

In the room, Breanna said, "Hop up on the bed and get

comfortable. The doctor is freshening up in his room. I'll go get him."

I nodded and climbed up onto the table. This was always my favorite part — the sonogram. I couldn't wait to meet my little boy, but I wanted him to stay inside all warm and cozy as long as he could. Not knowing what would happen to us once he wasn't inside of me anymore, I dreaded his birth day.

The door opened, and Breanna led the way before a man in a white coat with dark hair and sparkling brown eyes. My heart rate sped up, and I felt my pulse in my ears.

I jumped off the bed and ran over to the garbage can and emptied the contents of my stomach.

Still clutching the trash bin, I heard footsteps rush over to me. "Sadie, are you okay?"

Tilting my head upward, I stared into the eyes of the man I had married. The man I had loved. The man who had betrayed me. I said, "No. I am *not* okay."

35

MARTINA

"Hey, Hirsch, what's up?"

"We just got a break in the case."

"Which one?"

"The missing pregnant women. And I can't believe it, but it's the tip you gave me earlier from the Coast Guard. It turns out Daisy Hernandez and her parents met with a couple named Erica and Ben Benton. The parents came down and fingered the suspects from a photo array. The real identities of Erica and Ben Benton are none other than Breanna and Blaine Jarreau."

My jaw dropped. "I knew he was hiding something." But I hadn't imagined that.

"Yep. Now we need to meet with the DEA so we can get ahold of Breanna. In the meantime, I need to get ahold of Blaine."

"I'm sorry I'm not there to help you."

"I spoke with Sarge, and he plans to talk to the sheriff about you and Vincent. I need you back."

So many emotions. On one hand, I was thrilled for the lead on the case, but I felt horrible I had let Hirsch down when he needed me. And he did, more than ever, and so did those women. "Why don't you meet up with the DEA and see if they can pull Breanna without disturbing their other operation? In the meantime, go after Blaine."

That's what I would do if I hadn't been sidelined. Hirsch said, "I need to be careful."

"Yes, you do. Now that we know Breanna and Blaine are connected to organized crime, this could be very dangerous. Don't go after them alone."

"I won't."

Now, who's being the overprotective type? I didn't think I could recover from losing Hirsch because I hadn't been there to back him up. "Plus, you don't have evidence that they killed anybody. You only have eyewitness statement that they posed as parents willing to do an illegal adoption. Not enough for an arrest warrant, is it?"

"No, it's not."

"So, we have prime suspects with no evidence. How about if I watch Blaine? I could go to his office casually. Not official police business. Just to keep an eye on him."

"You're suspended, Martina."

"I'm not doing anything other than getting glitter stuck in my hair. And it's so hard to get out. Anyway, I can monitor him. If he tries to run, I'll call you. Nothing official, so no rules broken."

"I neither condone nor reject this idea."

That's a yes in my book. "Loud and clear. Thanks for letting me know what is going on."

"I'm not sure how I did this job without you. Now, it feels nearly impossible."

I felt the same way. "Let me see what I can do. I'll talk to Stavros. Maybe he can lend me some resources."

"I don't need or want any details, but I appreciate it."

I hung up the phone and glanced at the clock. It was late. But considering all I had done that day was work out at the gym and watch movies, I had a second wind. We needed eyes and ears on Blaine, and I would make sure we would get just that. Mom called out, "Dinner's ready."

After dinner, I would head out. "Okay, Mom, I'll be right there. I have to make a quick call."

She hollered back, "Okay."

I dialed the office. "Drakos Security and Investigations."

"Hi, Mrs. Pearson, this is Martina."

"Martina, so good to hear from you. How are you, dear?"

"I'm doing great. Is Stavros still in the office?"

"He is. Let me transfer you."

"Thank you." I had been suspended from the CoCo County Sheriff's Department, but that didn't mean I was suspended from my company. I was still an employee even though contracted to another organization. Hirsch needed help — the off-the-books kind of help — and Drakos would provide.

"This is Stavros."

"Hi, it's Martina."

"Twice in one day."

"I know. It's been a crazy day. And again, I'm sorry for you having to deal with Sarge, but the news story produced a huge break in the case." I paused. "But Hirsch's hands are tied because one of the prime suspects is tied up in a DEA investigation. The other is the husband of the missing person, which is how we came across the pregnant women. I need to look into the doctor's background and track his movements. The sheriff's department doesn't have enough evidence to arrest him, but I want eyes and ears on him at all times. I was hoping to use..."

Before I could finish, Stavros said, "Drakos resources?"

"Yes."

"Does Hirsch know about this?"

"I told him I'd monitor the doctor and that I was going to reach out to you for help. He said that's all he wanted to know."

"You got it, Martina. Research will help track this guy down."

"Thanks, Stavros."

"Anytime. I'll see you later."

I hung up the phone, feeling hopeful that not only could I help Hirsch but also get to the bottom of what happened to the missing pregnant women. I wasn't sure how they connected to Sadie, but my gut was telling me they did.

After dinner, I headed down to the offices of Drakos Security and Investigations. I waved at Mrs. Pearson, who gave me a wide smile outlined with her signature magenta lipstick. She stood up. "Oh, Martina, it's so good to see you." She gave me a light squeeze. I had known this woman almost my entire adult life. She'd seen me at my best and my worst.

"How is Zoey?"

"She's fantastic. She has been keeping busy with homework, drama, and her art."

"Oh, I miss seeing her beaming little face. You two have to come to the annual picnic this year."

"We will."

"Are you here to work?"

My backpack must have given me away. "I am."

"Are you coming back?"

"Temporarily." *Or not.* That was still TBD. There were worse outcomes.

"All right. It's late, so I'll let you get to it."

I said, "Have a good night," and headed back to my old stomping grounds toward Stavros's office. I waved.

"Well, Martina. It's good to see you."

"You too. I'm going over to Research to track movements for Blaine Jarreau. Breanna's a bit of a ghost and will be trickier since she's under DEA surveillance."

"If that's the case, stay away from that one, Martina. But go after Blaine."

"Will do." Likely, whatever Blaine was doing was connected to Breanna and the DEA. Once I found out enough about Blaine, I would tell Hirsch, and he could communicate with the DEA.

At that moment, my only concern was finding Blaine and understanding everything he was doing. We needed credit card movements, plane tickets purchased... the whole nine yards. I was glad we hadn't confronted Blaine with all the lies we had caught him in. He was completely oblivious that we were on to him and the secret he had been hiding.

36

HIRSCH

Alone, I greeted DEA Agents Spector and Florence. "Thank you, guys, for coming down."

"No problem. Sounds like you caught quite the break."

"I think we might have both caught a break. Please have a seat."

Because of the sensitive nature of the case, both the DEA and I felt it was better that we met face-to-face for developments relating to Breanna Jarreau.

Once we were seated across from each other, Agent Spector said, "We're all ears."

After briefing them on what we had learned about Breanna Jarreau and Blaine Jarreau's baby buying scheme, I said, "We've done as you asked and have stayed away from Breanna, but we need to know that you have eyes and ears on her as we build our case against those two. We will need to bring her in when we have enough evidence."

"We have eyes and ears on Breanna Jarreau. After we met last week, we dug deeper into her background and spoke with some of our informants. We think she's pretty deep within the Fuentes organization. So, if you have evidence she's good for murder and kidnapping, we can probably bring down Fuentes, too. Like I told you before, we know he's into drug trafficking, and that is what we had assumed the shipments were about. I'm not saying they're not smuggling drugs, but it sounds like maybe they were smuggling other things as well."

"Exactly. You have Breanna under surveillance, and we have Blaine, the brother, under surveillance. As soon as we collect more evidence, we should be in a good position to take them down."

"I agree. What's your plan?" Agent Spector asked.

"We have a private investigation firm keeping tabs on Blaine Jarreau's credit cards, airline reservations, and twenty-four-hour surveillance on his person — it's not officially sanctioned, but it's good enough to keep an eye on him."

"That's good, but I have to tell you, Hirsch, I still find it troubling because, like I said, after we met with you last week, we did a deep dive into Breanna Jarreau and yes, we see she has a brother who is a doctor, but we haven't found him connected to the Fuentes organization. We asked around and nobody's heard of him and nobody has seen him."

Agent Florence said, "If that's true, the theory that Breanna and Blaine are in on the baby trafficking scheme together doesn't totally hold up."

"That's the other thing. We haven't heard any whispers about baby trafficking either," Agent Spector added.

That was troubling. We didn't want to take down just Breanna. We wanted Blaine too. "Could it be that your informants only know about the drug business?"

"It's possible. We'll keep looking for a connection. It's obvious whatever Breanna was up to with these pregnant women wasn't good. And considering she's got the backing of Carlos Fuentes, she's got the funding for whatever her venture is. It could be that she's fairly high up in the organization and she's pulling all the strings. Maybe Fuentes doesn't know about the operation. He only cares about getting paid, so if he's making money, he might not be asking too many detailed questions. It doesn't mean we can't get him for it. As we investigate further, we'll let you know what we find."

Something didn't feel right about this. "It is strange that you have heard nothing about the doctor." Why hadn't they?

Agent Spector said, "If he's involved, we'll prove it."

"It was smart doing that press release," said Agent Florence.

I wasn't sure how to respond, considering the two members of our squad who were brave enough to do so had been suspended. "Unfortunately, not everybody in the department felt that way."

"No?"

Agent Spector's dark-bushy brows shot up. "It was a leak?"

"All I'll say is it wasn't sanctioned."

"Where's your partner, Martina? Is it her firm that's helping on the down low?" he asked with a smirk.

Clever DEA agents.

"She's on break from the sheriff's department, but yes, her firm is helping us out — as a favor."

Both agents nodded as if they understood to not ask any more questions. "We'll keep in touch. No worries about Breanna. We know exactly where she is at all times."

My phone buzzed.

"You can take that if you need to. We're about to head out anyhow."

They began packing up as I answered the call. "Hi, Martina."

"Hey, Hirsch. I just found something interesting. Blaine is going about his normal business work, home, work, home, but he just made a reservation for Thursday night on Southwest Airlines, Oakland to Seattle."

"He's leaving town again?" I raised my finger to stop the DEA agents.

"Looks like it."

"I wonder what is in Seattle? We know it's not a medical conference."

"I sure would like to find out. What are you doing Thursday night?" she asked, with a hint of mischief in her voice.

"Sounds like flying to Seattle."

"Hey, me too. What a coincidence."

"I'm just wrapping up with the DEA. Let's talk later about arrangements."

"You got it."

I set the phone down. "That was Martina. Blaine just made an airline reservation for a trip to Seattle. This is the second trip to Seattle this month. Last time we asked him about it, he said he was going to a medical conference. We checked it out. He wasn't registered for any medical conference."

"What's in Seattle?" Agent Spector asked.

"I don't know, but we plan to find out. My team and I will head up, see what he has going on up there. Maybe it's part of the organization. Maybe it's the missing piece to the entire thing."

"Keep us posted. If it's connected to the Fuentes organization, we can send some of our local DEA officers to help."

"That's much appreciated."

It was good to have backup from the DEA and Martina. Even if on the down low.

37

SADIE

Despite my protests, Blaine helped me back up to the hospital bed. "Everything's going to be okay, Sadie."

How do you figure? "How could you do this to me?"

He gave me a small grin. "Don't worry, everything will be fine. First things first. Let's look at our baby."

Speechless, I wanted to bite him. I wanted to claw at him. I wanted him to feel the way I felt. There was nothing that felt worse than his betrayal. Breanna, I had never been a fan of, but Blaine was my husband. The man who held my hand as we sat in the lobby of the fertility clinic month after month trying to create a family. The same man who held me tight as I cried because we weren't pregnant again. How could he have had his sister kidnap me and hold me hostage on a boat? For five months!

I glanced over at Breanna, who wore a satisfied look on her face. She was enjoying my anguish and obvious disgust for my husband. *Oh, is that how it is? I can play along with the best of them. Game on.* Once that witch was gone, Blaine and I were going to have a serious conversation. I wanted to know everything, and most of all, I wanted him to get me off that damn boat.

Blaine flicked on the machine and lifted my shirt. He squeezed the jelly onto my rather large belly before smoothing it over with the wand. It was the moment I had fantasized about since the day we had been married. That moment where we both were in the doctor's office, about to see our baby on the monitor for the first time.

He'd ruined it.

He'd ruined *everything*.

Our little guy's heartbeat sounded, and I stared at the screen. Even the wretched brother-sister duo couldn't ruin that moment for me. Our boy was beautiful and healthy.

Blaine was grinning from ear to ear.

Never could I have dreamed up the scenario in front of me. Blaine turned and gazed into my eyes. "He's perfect. Our baby boy is perfect."

I nodded slowly. Had Blaine lost his mind? Was that why all of this was happening? My mind raced. Did his approval of the baby mean they wouldn't kill me and take away our baby? Blaine must have been in contact with Breanna the whole time and had been the one ensuring I received everything I needed. This was actually good news. Not great news. My husband was a monster, after all. If they didn't kill me and take the baby, what would happen after he was born? Panic set in and I was over-come with emotion. Blaine put his hand on my arm. "Are you okay?"

Uh, no. Jerk face. "It's a lot to take in."

"I know, but it will all be okay."

Not believing a word out of the liar's mouth, I glanced back over at the screen to the image of my baby boy, who was moving around, blissfully unaware of our current situation.

Breanna said, "Well, it looks like everything is under control here. I'll go back up on deck and leave the two of you."

Blaine said, "Thank you, Bree."

Thank you?

Breanna said, "No problem, bro," and exited the birthing suite.

"You're behind all of this?"

"I had no idea you were pregnant. Why didn't you tell me?"

Looking at him with disbelief, I said, "That's why I went to the boat that day. I was setting up a dinner to tell you we were having a baby, and then there was a man with a gun and a pregnant woman who was crying in the stateroom."

He shut his eyes as if he hadn't known the gravity of the mistake he had made.

"What have you done?" I cried.

"It's not what you think."

"Oh, no? Because I think you and your evil sister have been kidnapping pregnant women and stealing their babies and then killing the women. I've met two already! Are you going to do the same to me?"

When Blaine had started working long hours, my best friend was sure Blaine was cheating, and I believed her. He had a second cell phone that I found, but there weren't any names, just phone numbers on it. He was out at all hours and would say he was working. All sure signs of infidelity, but I was wrong, wasn't I?

He said, "They didn't know who you were when they took you."

"And that would have made a difference?"

"Yes, if they knew you were my wife, they would've let you go."

Now I know he's lost his mind. "Breanna knows I'm your wife, and I've been trapped on this boat for five months!"

"They didn't know at first. It all started when Breanna had the idea of going into the adoption business. She knew how hard of a time we had and that there were other families going through the same thing. We would be like matchmakers for babies and families. The regular route, as you know, could take years, but this way, we could match families in a small fraction of that time. For a fee, of course."

None of that explained why I had been held captive. "So, you figured you'd kidnap and murder pregnant women for a profit?"

"No, that's not how it started. Everything went wrong. It wasn't supposed to be like that. It's not what you think, I swear. Look, I can't talk about that right now."

What was I supposed to think? With tears streaming down my face, I said, "Why have you kept me here? I want off this boat!"

Footsteps sounded toward the suite, and a knock shifted his attention from me to the door. "You just have to trust me. I promise everything will be okay. I'm working on a plan."

Trust him? How could I possibly ever trust him again?

Breanna entered the suite. "How is everything going in here?"

Blaine grinned. "Everything is great. I'm going to be a father, and you're going to be an auntie."

Her face twisted. "I can't wait. You'll have to think about names."

The exchange between them led me to believe there was a lot more to the story. Breanna didn't seem to trust Blaine, and there was no hiding the fact she couldn't care less she was about to become an auntie. How was it possible that this situation was even more confusing than before?

Feeling a little dizzy, I leaned back on the bed.

Breanna said, "You look tired, Sadie. Perhaps we should leave you to get some rest."

Tired? Yes, I was tired. I was tired of the betrayal and the death and of the stupid boat. Nodding, I shut my eyes and tried to forget that my husband was a murderer and a liar. That he and his freak of a sister were trafficking stolen babies. Was continuing their bloodline a good idea? Was my baby cursed? No, he wasn't just a Jarreau. He was part of me too, and I knew I had to get my baby as far away from them as humanly possible — for both of our sakes.

38

MARTINA

SEARCHING OVERHEAD FOR MY SEAT ASSIGNMENT, I FOUND it and shoved my carry-on into the overhead bin before taking my seat next to the tall, well-built, blond-haired man. "Do I know you from somewhere?"

Hirsch chuckled. "You're Martina, right?"

"I am. What a coincidence."

"Indeed."

The sheriff had refused to let me come back to the CoCo County Sheriff's Department, despite the break in the case because of the news story. Thankfully, I had backup working for my firm. Stavros assured me I would still receive my regular paycheck, whether the sheriff's department paid out my contract or not. It was always good to have backup. Plus, there was nothing in my contract or stipulation of my temporary suspension that said I couldn't work other cases or any case, really. And Hirsch and I just happened to decide to go to Seattle at the same time. At least that was our cover story, not that anyone would believe it, but how could they disprove it?

Hirsch and I had made flight reservations for Thursday morning to arrive in Seattle before Blaine Jarreau's plane landed. We couldn't find any property records or hotel reservations in Blaine's name, so we had to find out where he was staying the old-fashioned way. Once we spotted him, we would follow him and find out where he went.

Hirsch was on the job for the sheriff's department. I was on the job for my security and investigations firm. It was a lot like the first time we worked together. We had teamed up but worked for two different organizations with one common goal. The only difference in this case was that Hirsch and I were friends.

According to Hirsch, the sheriff was pretty ticked off about the press leak. Even though it may be the reason we were able to solve the case which would give the sheriff's department great publicity. Sheriff Lafontaine was a huge fan of anything that made him look good. So why was he still up in a tizzy?

"You ever been to Seattle before?" I asked.

"I have. You?"

"A few times. Once for work and once for pleasure."

The work trip involved interviewing my client's ex-husband since she was being stalked and had suspected her ex was behind the whole thing. Turned out he wasn't the stalker after all, so the trip had only given me insight into a veritable monster who believed he had owned his ex-wife. The other time was with Jared, when we were young and in love and exploring the city, having the time of our lives. This was my third trip to Seattle, perhaps giving me new memories to think about the next time I returned. "How's the wedding planning?"

"It's going. I took your advice and surprised Kim with a spa certificate for this weekend."

"Was she pleased?" I asked.

He grinned. "You know she was."

I smiled. "Don't you have cake tasting this weekend?"

"I do. I am definitely looking forward to that. Hey, don't you have some big plans of your own this weekend?"

Don't remind me. "Yep. I have a date with Dave."

"Are you excited?"

"I don't know. Maybe more like nervous."

"Martina Monroe, nervous?"

"I mean, it's like a job interview, right? You used to date before you found the love of your life. You know what it's like."

Hirsch nodded. "It's not for the faint of heart. You're tough. You'll survive. What night?"

"Saturday."

"What's the plan?"

"Dinner followed by bowling."

Hirsch chortled. "Bowling. Was that his idea?"

"Yep. It's not the worst idea I've ever heard. It's the end of January and cold out, so any kind of activity would have to be indoors. It will give us a chance to talk to each other versus sitting quietly in a movie theater."

"That's a good point. You much of a bowler?"

"No." I hadn't bowled since I was in high school. I wondered if Zoey would like to bowl. She and Kaylee would probably enjoy it, especially since there were snacks for sale including soda, fries, burgers, basically junk food, which was her favorite.

When she was younger, she wanted to do everything I did, including making sure there was enough protein at breakfast or whole grains with lunch. As she was getting older, she had her own taste in music, activities, and food. It was only a matter of time before she was a grown-up. I lowered my voice. "Let's talk strategy for when he arrives."

"Sounds good."

For the rest of the flight, Hirsch and I went back and forth on the different things we could do to get ahold of Blaine. It was mostly my firm tracking his movements, considering in

the world of law enforcement, you needed warrants and probable cause for those kinds of things. Truth was, we had
nothing concrete on Blaine other than a witness who said he
tried to adopt her daughter's baby. It didn't exactly prove
murder or kidnapping, especially since Daisy's body was never
found.

We knew his sister was bad to the bone, and he was secretly
in contact with her. If my gut was right, he also knew exactly
what happened to his wife, and it was somehow mixed up with
the Fuentes crime organization.

After a safe landing, we headed to the local Starbucks
within the airport to get caffeinated. I said, "Okay, his plane
arrives in forty-five minutes. Let's get coffee and then split up."

Hirsch would pick up the rental car while I stuck around
the terminal to get visual confirmation. We would communicate
via cell phone and track him separately until we met up again.

"Perfect."

We advanced in line. "I'll have a tall black coffee."

Hirsch said, "And I'll have the caramel macchiato."

I glanced back at Hirsch and shook my head, defeated. I
didn't think I was ever going to get him off the sugar and cream.

After paying for the order, we waited and surveyed our
surroundings to see where all the exits were.

"I'll stay at the rental car agency while you follow him
there."

"You got it, boss," I said teasingly, but then it reminded me of
Vincent. He was now on his third day of suspension, and I felt
terrible about that. I didn't know how I could cope if he lost his
job. Although, for someone with his talent, we could always hire
him at Drakos Security & Investigations, but I knew he enjoyed
working at the sheriff's department, and that was likely his first
choice.

Coffee in hand, Hirsch and I went our separate ways. I

headed toward the board and checked the gate number for Blaine's flight. *On time. Arrival in thirty-five minutes.*

Hoping Blaine wouldn't recognize me, I pulled out my black cap and tugged it on. Blaine knew my face, so I grabbed the magazine from my backpack and planted myself in a seat. Flipping through pages, I peered above to monitor the crowd. It was entirely possible somebody would be meeting Blaine. Although, not likely considering he rented a car.

Thirty minutes later, Blaine's flight arrived, and passengers slowly emerged from the gate one by one. I put away my magazine, stood up, and hurried behind a pillar, hiding myself. I pulled out my cell phone and dialed Hirsch. "The plane is disembarking now."

"I'll stay on the line."

Glancing up, I caught sight of Blaine. I looked away and whispered, "He's here."

"Okay, I'll meet you at the rental car station."

I hung up and followed Blaine down the escalator toward ground transportation and rental cars. I didn't think he spotted me, but he wasn't on the lookout either. For somebody who had a lot to hide, he sure was unaware of his surroundings. Luckily, the airport was busy enough, and it was easy to fall behind several other passengers while monitoring the back of Blaine.

He approached the shuttle stop, and I thought, *This is where it will be a little tricky.*

Three passengers behind Blaine in line for the shuttle to the rental agency. I didn't think he noticed me, as he was busy fiddling with something in his duffel bag.

The shuttle arrived, and the doors opened. I watched as Blaine took a seat in the front, so I took a seat in the back by the door, obscuring his view of me.

My heart beat faster as the adrenaline gave me energy and fired up my nerves.

He got off at the Thrifty car rental stop. After he departed, I lowered my cap and hopped off the bus. I hurried in the opposite direction of the rental counter and pulled out my phone. "I'm here."

"I see him. I'm to the right in the white Ford Focus."

I hung up my phone and jogged over to Hirsch. He popped the trunk, and I threw in my suitcase. Inside the car, I said, "The eagle has landed."

Hirsch nodded with a slight smile.

"How long did it take you to get the car?"

"They're pretty fast. No more than ten minutes."

"All right. We'll sit tight and follow him as soon as he gets on the road."

Hirsch said, "No hotel reservations means he's going somewhere familiar."

"Yep. He must know somebody who lives here. But who? We didn't find any records for anybody in his family, so not one of the Jarreaus. Maybe a girlfriend? Maybe he's had a secret mistress all along."

"It would explain the secrecy. Kind of."

"His wife has been missing for five years. If he had a girlfriend, nobody would blame him. Yet, he chose to lie to us."

"Exactly."

I tapped Hirsch on the shoulder. "Okay, he's getting into the black Ford Taurus."

Hirsch nodded. "Let's do this."

After several hours on the highway, I couldn't help wondering where in the heck Blaine was going. Somewhere not in Seattle proper. Maybe not even in Washington?

Hirsch said, "Look at the sign. The ferry terminal is close to here. Maybe he's taking a ferry to an island off the coast?"

Sure enough, we followed Blaine as he drove toward the ferry to Orcas Island. What I understood about the island was that it was sparsely populated. There were only a few restaurants and not much else other than whale watching and some shops for seafood and other treats.

"This is actually good, Hirsch."

"Why is that?"

"Orcas Island isn't very big. We could probably pull records for all the properties."

"I guess, but in time to figure out where he's going?"

"I'll see what I can do." I dialed in the request to the awesome research team at Drakos Security & Investigations and then placed my phone in my backpack. As we waited to get onto the ferry, I was thankful we had fueled up on coffee before Blaine arrived, and I had a backpack full of bananas and protein bars.

39

SADIE

Pacing the top deck, I tried to minimize the fury burning inside of me. My rage toward my husband, my sister-in-law, and this godforsaken boat needed to be contained until I could escape. Blaine had stayed on the boat with me for two weeks and promised to stay until the baby was born. He swore up and down that everything would be okay, and he was working on a plan to keep all of us safe and together. At that point, I believed about two percent of the words that came out of his mouth.

I was suspecting he was on board to ensure the baby's safety and not mine. Would he take my baby away from me and then off me like the others? Maybe it's all he wanted, anyway. For all I knew, he had been cheating, and he planned to steal my baby and live a new life with a new Mrs. Blaine Jarreau.

Or was he sincere and really looking for a solution out of this? If that were true, why had he waited so long to rescue us?

I had been playing nice since he'd been on the boat, not wanting either of them to think I was angry or that I would run the very second I had the chance. *Oh, but I would run — as fast as my body would allow.* The only thing I was certain about was that I was safe as long as I was pregnant. But what about when I wasn't?

Blaine approached with a wide smile. "Hi, honey. How are you feeling?"

Honey. "Pretty good."

"No contractions yet?"

It was like he couldn't wait to get rid of me. "Not yet." And as if the universe was playing a cruel trick on me, a stabbing pain hit me in the abdomen. I cried out and hunched over, gripping my belly. Blaine rushed over to hold me so I wouldn't topple off the boat. It passed, and I stood up with Blaine's arm still around me.

"Was that a contraction?"

"I think so."

With glee in his eyes, he said, "We're having a baby, Sadie."

"I can't wait to see his little face." It was true. I was dying to meet my baby boy. Blaine and I had already picked out a name. Not that Blaine deserved to pick out the name of our baby. As soon as I was free, I was done with him *forever*.

"We should get you downstairs. It's not safe up here."

I hid my eye roll and followed him down to the stateroom below.

"Do you want to go to the birthing suite or back to your room?"

"My room."

What if I needed a Cesarean or an emergency blood transfusion? Were they prepared? If they were, maybe they had a scalpel I could get my hands on. Would I be willing to kill them for mine and my baby's freedom? I stared into Blaine's dark-brown eyes, and I knew the answer.

Absolutely.

"Let's get you comfortable, okay?"

I said, "You're too good to me," and had to suppress a laugh.

Too good to me? He and his demented sister were holding me captive on a boat.

"Can I get you anything? Ice chips?"

Off this boat? "No, I'm okay. Thank you."

"Just in case, I'll go get you some. I'll be right back."

Of course, Blaine always knew best.

I smiled sweetly and watched him leave.

Even if I was willing to kill Blaine and his psycho sister to get free, there was still the man with the gun. Could I really take them all out in my current state? It wasn't likely. Unless... I could tap into Blaine's softer side. It had to still be there, at least a little.

When we met, he was warm and kind. He had remained that way throughout our marriage, until the last year, when I guessed he was killing women and selling their children. Why did he do it? We didn't need the money. Why wouldn't he tell me how all of this started and ended with me? Was he afraid of prison? His sister? As much as my hatred burned for him, his involvement still didn't sit right.

EIGHT HOURS LATER, I WAS CRADLING MY NEWBORN SON IN my arms. He cooed and wiggled, and I was so in love.

Breanna asked, "What are you going to name him?"

Blaine spoke for me. *Go figure.* "Zachary Charles."

"How wonderful. You know, Blaine, I think he kinda looks like you."

Poor baby. Not that Blaine was a bad-looking man. He wasn't. But the fewer of his father's traits he inherited, the better.

Had our entire relationship been a lie? Who was this new Blaine? I didn't like him.

Breanna left with the crew to give us new family time. I stared into Blaine's eyes, clutching at our child. *Out of options, the time is now or never.* "You have to get us out of here. We can't stay on this boat forever."

Blaine nodded as he ran his finger down Zachary's cheek. "I've been working on a plan. You'll have to change your name. You can never reach out to your family or friends, and eventually I'll join you. We have to make it look realistic."

I shook my head. "I don't understand."

"I will set up a new life for you. We'll have to start completely from scratch. It's the only way we'll survive this. Sadie, I know I don't deserve your trust or your love anymore. But..." He paused and gazed at Zachary and then back at me. "We're a family, and I need to protect all of us."

"How? When?"

"I'm still working on it. It might take some time, and I may need to adjust if it becomes too dangerous. First, I need to convince Breanna to bring you on land, so I can put you in a safe house. Her men will guard it, but at least you won't be on this boat anymore. Unfortunately, you can't contact anybody, and you can't talk to strangers. Basically, it'll be..."

"Like I'm still a prisoner?"

He nodded. "But I'll be able to visit with you and the baby."

Oh, yeah. That's exactly what I want — more time with Blaine, my murdering, baby stealing, lying creep of a husband. "Land would be better, and getting to see you will be nice." I hadn't given up hope yet.

"Take some time. I promise, one day this will be a memory. A distant memory."

I smiled at him and said, "You're right. We're a family now. I trust you."

He leaned in and gave me a light kiss on the forehead.

He wasn't the only one who could lie through their teeth.

40

HIRSCH

Successfully parked on the ferry, I called our contacts at the DEA. "Agent Spector."

"Agent Spector, this is Hirsch."

"Hirsch, how is it going out there?"

"We have sights on Blaine. We're on a ferry to Orcas Island, Washington."

"What the heck could he be hiding on Orcas Island?"

"You know the place?"

"My family likes to vacation there. I'm originally from Washington state. There aren't a lot of places to hide on the island. There are only a few hotels, restaurants, and a lot of outdoor activities like kayaking and boating. But my guess is Blaine's not going there for recreation. He's going there to see someone who is in hiding."

"Are there a lot of rentals on the island?"

"I would guess so. It's mostly a resort island, with probably less than five thousand full and part-time residents. It's not even fifty-eight square miles. Like I said, there's not a lot of hiding spots."

"Good to know. I'll let you know when we figure out where he is going."

"All right, I'll call the Seattle team and have them ready to move in. There is a small airfield on the island. If we need to get there in a pinch, we can."

It's great to have backup with extensive resources. "When I have more details, I'll call you."

I hung up and explained to Martina what Spector had told me.

"What if...?"

"What if what?" I asked.

"If Blaine has visited the island a couple of times just this month, there must be something pretty important here, right?"

"Yes, and we should look at travel records for Blaine and Breanna to see when the visits started."

"Not a bad idea."

Martina called her firm.

What was Blaine hiding on the island?

The ferry docked, and Martina hung up her phone. "My team is on it. They'll start digging."

I nodded as I peered ahead. It was slow moving off the ferry, and I worried I might lose Blaine, but soon I saw there was only one direction out of the ferry area on what looked like a two-lane road. Wherever Blaine was going, we would learn soon enough, especially since the island was less than fifty-eight square miles big.

Three vehicles behind Blaine, we followed him for over ten minutes before we were alone on the road lined with blue ocean, green trees, and stormy skies. It was obvious why people would vacation on the island. It was stunning.

Blaine took a left down a desolate road. We were pretty obvious, but at that point, I was going to have to risk it. We were too deep to duck out. It was possible we would step into the

Fuentes crime organization's secret headquarters, but Martina and I were already in Kevlar and armed. Not that we would go in with guns blazing. Martina had been shot twice since we had been working together. She wouldn't take a hit again — at least, not on my watch. We'd be smart and call for backup first, but in case things turned sideways, we were ready. Considering the remote nature of the island, it would be a great spot for a drug lord to hide. Blaine made another turn down a side road made of gravel. Likely private. I pulled over and stopped the car. "We should go on foot from here."

Without a word, we exited the vehicle and hurried down the side of the road. I stared down the gravel driveway lined with a grove of trees. At the end stood a small house situated amongst the natural beauty. Blaine parked out front and I turned around. "I'll call the DEA with the address, and you call your team to figure out who owns this place."

"I'm on it."

"Spector, it's Hirsch. We followed Blaine to 2340 Rosario Road, E Sound, Washington."

"Nestled in the trees?"

"It is."

"Any movement in the house? Any sign of Fuentes or other men?"

I stepped closer to the driveway. "I don't think so. The house isn't big. Maybe two-thousand square feet, two-story. Modest."

"Might be a vacation rental."

"Martina's crew is pulling property records now."

"Good. I have a feeling you're onto something there. I'll tell the team in Seattle the address."

"As soon as I have visual of anyone else, I'll call."

"Great. We'll stand down until we get notification or if you don't call back in fifteen minutes."

"I appreciate that."

Waiting for Martina to end her call, I watched the front of the house. It was a green two-story with white trim. Behind the house was some type of structure. I ran across to the other side of the street to get a better look. With the structure in my sights, I stepped back and processed what I had seen.

Martina hurried over. "What do you see?"

"What does that look like up there?"

She tilted her head. "You've got to be kidding. That's a kids' play structure."

"That's what I thought."

"My team said the house is registered as a vacation rental, but it hasn't been listed in several years."

"Odd." What was going on in that house?

"I'm having my team contact the owners to see who's staying in it."

"Good idea. The DEA is on standby."

"Nice."

A flash of movement toward the back of the house caught my attention. "Over there. What's that?"

"That's a kid."

Sure enough, I could see him now. The boy was running around, and Blaine appeared to be chasing him. "A secret love child?"

Martina said, "A secret something."

"I'm guessing it's not the drug headquarters for Carlos Fuentes."

"I'm guessing not. We should approach."

I nodded and hurried down the steps. As we were walking down the drive, the little boy and Blaine ran toward the front of the house, oblivious to their two visitors, until the little boy stopped and pointed. "Who's that?"

Blaine looked up, and our eyes locked. Blaine grabbed the little boy's hand. "They're visitors, Zach."

"Who are they?"

I said, "Hello, Blaine, we have some questions for you."

"Are they your friends, Daddy?"

Martina and I exchanged glances. "Daddy?"

Blaine slowly shut his eyes and shook his head. "Yes, this is my son."

Performing mental mathematics, I stared at the boy. He was about five, adorable, and a perfect mix of Sadie and Blaine. Had Sadie been pregnant, after all? Did Blaine kill her and then keep the child? Who was taking care of Zach?

Martina knelt down in front of the little boy.

"Hi, Zach, my name is Martina."

The boy smiled brightly. "Hi."

"Is your mommy home?"

Before the little boy could respond, Blaine said, "I can explain."

41

SADIE

Like every other morning for the last three and half years, I waved to our guard, who was disguised as landscaping staff. Blaine had promised the guards and the seclusion were temporary. He had said he was working toward a new life for us. One that allowed us to work and go to school and live normal lives — under assumed names. Wouldn't you know it? But nearly four years later, I was still a prisoner. He swore it was because Breanna thought we would go to the authorities and that there were others in her organization who wanted me dead. But, considering I hadn't trusted Blaine since the day I set eyes on him on that boat, I didn't believe anything he said. If living at gunpoint wasn't bad enough, I also had to pretend I loved Blaine and that I was his adoring wife and that I trusted him and wanted to be with him. It was eating away at my soul, but it was what I had to do for my son. If only I could get him to lose the guard, Zach and I could make our escape.

Breanna and Blaine were planning a visit that day to celebrate my son's fourth birthday. There was no question, if it weren't for Zach, I would be a goner. They probably would have shot me and then buried my body so nobody would ever find me or know what had happened to me. Zach had saved my life in so many ways. It was silly to wish my original plan had worked and that instead of armed kidnappers who had arrived on the boat that day, it would have been Blaine. We would have had a nice dinner, and I would have shared the news that we were going to be parents. Oh, how time changed my view of things. Like the idea of romantic love and a warm, caring family.

I supposed I should be grateful that they hadn't killed me, and they hadn't stolen my baby like I believed they had done to those other women. I couldn't bear to think of how many were taken after I was gone. The whole situation disgusted me.

The isolation was a bit maddening. I missed talking to other people. Working. Having a life outside of the house. It was a sizable property where Zach and I would play outside for hours when the weather was nice. When it snowed, we took the sleds out. Blaine visited a few times a month, and Zach was always so happy when Daddy came home.

That didn't mean I wouldn't slit Blaine's throat if it meant we would be free.

Blaine had to know this arrangement couldn't last forever. Zach was four years old and should be in preschool with kids his own age. He should be learning how to form friendships and sharing and caring about other people. This was no way to raise a child. Eventually, Zach would have questions. Questions I couldn't answer without giving away his daddy and Auntie Breanna's secrets.

Waving to Zach, who was climbing up the steps to the slide, I beamed at my pride and joy. He called out, "Mommy, Mommy. Look!"

"Wow! Look at you!"

The light of my life squealed in delight as he slid down the slide. The sound of tires on gravel alerted me that our party guests had arrived. *Oh, joy, the Jarreau psychopaths are on the island.*

Zach ran up to me. "Daddy?"

"Yes. Daddy and Auntie Breanna are visiting today to celebrate your birthday."

"Yeah!" Zach punched his arms in the air and jumped up and down as only a four-year-old would.

Blaine exited the truck and ran over to us. He gave me a light peck on the cheek and then kneeled down to scoop up his son. "Happy birthday, Zach."

"Daddy!"

It would be difficult to take Blaine away from his son. As much as I resented him, I couldn't deny the love Zach had for him. I prayed our freedom wasn't dependent on Blaine's death. Breanna was a different story. I didn't think anyone would miss her. "Hi, Breanna."

"Hi, Sadie, how are you?" she asked with a fake smile.

"I'm great. Thank you." *As great as any prisoner could be.*

She knelt down to be eye level with Zach. "Happy birthday, Zach."

"Thank you, Auntie!"

She gave him a hug as if she were capable of love. I knew it was a disguise. Nobody who did what Breanna did could be capable of actual human emotions, like empathy and love.

Once the hugs and greetings were out of the way, Zach faced his visitors. "Mommy made cake with sprinkles," he explained in his best four-year-old speech.

Blaine said, "That sounds amazing. I can't wait. Are there birthday candles too?"

Zach bobbed his head and then held up four fingers.

"That's right, Zach. You're four now. Such a big boy."

Zach grabbed Blaine's hand and led him into the house. I smiled at Breanna and followed my loving husband and child inside. I didn't need to converse with Breanna any more than I absolutely had to. As far as I was concerned, she was the devil.

After cake and presents, Zach was down for his nap, and I was alone with Blaine. I said, "Can you believe he's ours?"

"I still can't," he said with a smile.

"He's amazing and bright."

"That he is. He's perfect."

Shifting to a more serious tone, I said, "You know we can't stay like this forever. He needs to be in school next year and to be around kids his own age. He has asked questions about the gardener and the handyman. This can't keep going on. What is the plan, Blaine?"

"I agree with you, but the only way to do it is if we all disappear without a hint of us running away. I don't have enough money yet."

That was what he had told me four years ago, and my patience had grown thin. "What if Zach and I go first? When you have enough money to leave your practice, you can join us."

He shook his head. "No. She'll know I hid you and have me killed. I'm thinking Breanna doesn't trust me anymore. She isn't happy about this arrangement at all."

"Are you happy with this arrangement?" I asked.

"No, but you're safe, and so is Zach. That's what's most important."

"We need to get out of here."

"I'm working on it. It's going to take some time."

"We're running out of time."

Breanna sauntered into the kitchen. "What are you two lovebirds talking about?"

"Just how we can't believe we have an adorable four-year-old child," I said with motherly pride.

Breanna said, "It is a bit of a miracle. What else were you talking about?"

Blaine said, "It's not any of your concern."

He may be correct in assuming she didn't trust him anymore.

"It is my business. It affects my life and my livelihood."

She is still murdering women.

"She's my wife, and he's my child. They are my number one priority."

"You need to recheck your priorities, Blaine. You do what I say, or we both go to jail — or worse."

"Is that a threat?" Blaine asked with fury in his eyes.

"Yes. He has threatened my life and yours."

Who is he?

"Breanna, I could blow this whole thing up if I wanted to. It's all your fault. It's because of you we're even in this predicament."

"Don't get so sanctimonious with me, brother. You were involved from the beginning."

"Yeah, and I wanted to stop. You blackmailed me into keeping your secrets!"

"You could have gone to the authorities and turned yourself in at any time. You're a coward," she spat.

"You better watch it."

Breanna whipped out a gun from behind her. "Or what?"

I clutched Blaine, amazed I still saw him as a protector. But despite my feelings of rage toward him, it was what he had been doing — protecting me and protecting Zach.

Blaine said, "Calm down."

"I am calm. You're with me or you're against me. You need to pick a side."

"Or what?"

"You're both dead, and I'll sell your little boy."

Blaine turned bright red, and his nostrils flared. He shoved me off him as he lunged at Breanna.

A loud bang sounded in my ears.

Lying on the floor, I tried to understand what was happening, but all I could hear was, "Sadie! Can you hear me? Sadie! Stay with me!" before I fell into unconsciousness.

42

MARTINA

"Let's hear it, Blaine."

"This is Zach. He is my son. He's Sadie's and my son."

"Sadie was pregnant?"

"I didn't know it at the time. I swear, I didn't."

"What happened, Blaine? Where is Sadie?" I asked.

The little boy said, "Sadie. Mommy," with glee in his eyes.

As if on cue, the front door of the house creaked open, and a woman stepped onto the porch. She had long, flowing blonde hair and bright blue eyes. The little boy turned around and pointed. "Mommy." He ran toward Sadie Jarreau. What had we just walked into? There was no way this could be the same as the Anastasia and Ryder Hall missing persons case, right? Were Blaine and Sadie connected to the Italian mob?

We followed the little boy toward Sadie. "Ma'am, are you Sadie Jarreau?"

"Yes, who are you?"

"My name's Detective Hirsch, and this is my partner, Martina Monroe. We've been looking for you."

"You have?"

I said, "Yes, we have, and we questioned your husband

several times about your whereabouts. He swore up and down that he didn't know where you were."

Tears streamed down Sadie's cheeks. "Because he and his psychotic sister have been keeping me here," she said through gritted teeth.

"Blaine, have you been keeping Sadie against her will?"

He looked at Sadie, his son, and back at us. "I want a lawyer." Sadie knelt down and clutched her son, tears streaming down her face.

The little boy asked, "Why are you crying?"

"They're happy tears, honey. Happy tears."

"Happy?"

Sadie nodded.

Why had Blaine held her hostage on Orcas Island? None of this made any sense.

Hirsch said, "Ma'am, are there any weapons in the house? Knives. Guns. That sort of thing?"

"We have kitchen knives, but nothing else. No guns."

"Blaine, do you have any weapons on you?" Hirsch asked.

"No."

I glanced over at the boy and Sadie. It would scar him for life to watch his dad get handcuffed in front of him. But then again, he had been held prisoner his whole life. It could be worse.

Hirsch looked at me. "I need to call the DEA, and then I'll take Blaine into the house and question him. Why don't you stay out here and talk to Sadie about what the heck has been going on?"

"You got it."

"Everyone, stay where you are. I'll be back in a minute," he said, before walking a few paces away to make his call.

Zach looked worried as he clung to his mother's arm. I said, "Zach, how old are you now?"

He held up his hand.

"Five?"

He nodded.

"Wow. A big boy! I have a daughter. She's ten years old."

Zach's hazel eyes widened. "What's her name?"

"Her name is Zoey."

"Does she have a dog? I really want a dog."

"She does. His name is Barney, and he loves to play in the backyard."

"He has a ball?"

"He has three!"

Zach smiled.

Hirsch returned. "Okay, Blaine, I need you to come with me."

He didn't put up a fuss but refused to talk. They went inside the house, and I stared into Sadie's bright blue eyes. "Are you okay?"

"I think I am now."

"Is there somewhere we can sit and talk?"

"We have a table out back. Zach can play as we talk."

"Sounds good." I followed her and the little boy as he skipped along, holding his mom's hand as they entered their backyard. The yard was outfitted with a table and chairs, a barbecue pit, a jungle gym, and a toy car. Zach had a nice life, albeit a secluded one.

About to sit, I noticed Sadie shiver. "Did you want to get a blanket?" She was already wearing a down jacket, but the breeze had a chill to it.

"I'll be fine, thank you."

We sat. Sadie said, "Zach, do you want to play in the jungle gym? I need to talk to Ms. Monroe. Just grown-ups, okay?"

He nodded.

"Stay where I can see you."

He said, "Okay," and ran off.

As Zach climbed up the ladder to the slide, I said, "Sadie, Detective Hirsch and I work for the CoCo County Sheriff's Department in the Cold Case Division. We came across your missing persons case, filed by your best friend May. Amanda, May's sister, is dating one of our squad members. May asked him to ask the squad to reopen your case and find out what really happened to you."

Sadie wiped her eyes that were glowing pink from the tears. "May. The best friend I ever had. I've missed her so much. This whole thing has been such a nightmare. If it wasn't for Zach, I don't know what I would have done."

"What happened, Sadie? Have you been here this whole time?"

"No, I haven't."

I listened in awe as Sadie recounted her abduction, her time with Rosa and Janine, and the shocking realization that her sister-in-law Breanna was the boss and then her husband showing up five months into her captivity on the yacht.

Incredible.

"How did you get off the yacht and end up here?"

"Blaine said it was temporary. He said he wanted to hide me, but Breanna wouldn't allow it. He said she would kill all of us if we tried to run. She allowed me to live here, only if we were guarded."

"Where are the guards now?"

"They left an hour ago, to catch the ferry. They only leave us alone when Blaine or Breanna come to visit." Sadie glanced over to her son, who was happily playing in his back yard.

"Did you ever ask to leave?"

Sadie laughed, bitterly. "Every time he visited. He kept telling me to be patient. I swear, when I married him, I never thought he was capable of this."

"Do you know what Blaine had been involved in?"

"He told me his only involvement was delivering the babies on the yacht. He never killed anyone. So he said. I no longer trust anything he says to me."

"Do you know what they did with the babies?"

"They wouldn't tell me, but I assumed they were selling them or something just as bad."

"Do you know what Breanna's role in this was?"

"Other than being the devil? She was the boss. All the guards took orders from her. She's a total psychopath. She tried to kill me. Twice."

"She tried to kill you? When was this?"

"The first time was when I was on the yacht. She stood next to the guard, giving the order to shoot me, I assumed to keep me quiet about what I had seen. When he raised the weapon, I shouted out that I was pregnant. She called off the shooter and then held me captive. The second time was on Zach's fourth birthday."

"I'm so sorry you've had to go through all of this. Do you know why she tried to kill you on Zach's birthday?"

"She swears it was an accident. She was fighting with Blaine, and she pulled out a gun. He rushed her, and the next thing I knew, she had shot me. I thought all of my efforts to keep us safe were in vain. But Blaine mended me back to health. Luckily, the gunshot was a through and through. It hurt like heck, but I recovered. I'm still here and you know what? I never gave up hope. Some would've by now, but I hadn't. Thank you, Ms. Monroe. Thank you for finding me and for finding my son. I just want my life back."

I wished I could assure Sadie she was safe, but I wasn't too sure. "Did you know who Breanna was working with?"

"No."

"We've partnered with the DEA and have found that

Breanna is working with some terrible people. Did you meet any of these other people she works with? Any Latino men or women?"

"There were the guards, men with guns, and the helpers who helped with food and in the delivery room. I got the impression they all worked for Breanna. Is there someone else higher up than Breanna? That would make sense."

Sadie had likely never met or seen Carlos Fuentes, but she knew about the operation and that could put her safety at risk. "We believe so."

Sadie turned serious. "We could still be in danger."

"We'll keep you safe." We would have to create a plan for that.

Hirsch entered the backyard with Blaine, who had his wrists cuffed together. "How's it going?" I asked.

Hirsch said, "The DEA is on their way," and then told Blaine to sit down on the chair.

"Sadie has been telling me everything that has happened from the time they abducted her until now. Blaine and Breanna have been holding her captive and Breanna shot her."

Hirsch turned to Blaine and shook his head.

I added, "She didn't meet anybody other than Breanna and her staff."

"I'm sure the DEA can use any information she can provide."

I nodded.

Sadie turned to Blaine. "I can't believe you did this to us, Blaine. To your own son."

"She would've killed me and you and the baby. Don't you get that? And I only kept you here so you would be safe. I know Bree is crazy. I wish I had stayed away from her. She's always been rotten."

Was that true? Had Blaine been strong-armed by his sister?

Was she the criminal mastermind forcing him to do this? Something didn't feel right about that. "Is that right, Blaine? We met with a witness who said that you and Breanna met with her daughter, Daisy, and were planning to buy her baby, and then she disappeared."

Blaine lowered his eyes.

"Is it true?" Hirsch asked.

"There was never a plan to hurt Daisy. Sadie and I couldn't conceive and thought maybe adoption would be the right route, but it's quite difficult to adopt. When we saw Daisy at the restaurant, and she told us she was giving the baby up for adoption, Bree had the idea of buying it from her. I knew it wasn't exactly legal, but I knew we'd give the baby a wonderful home, plus we would compensate her financially. It was a win-win. I was going to surprise Sadie, but then..."

"And then what happened?" Hirsch asked.

"Daisy changed her mind. I was disappointed but knew it was too good to be true anyway, but then it all went wrong. I should've known better than to think Bree would just walk away. That poor girl." Blaine lowered his head and raised his cuffed hands to his face as he cried.

"All wrong how?" Hirsch asked.

Hirsch looked at me.

I nodded.

Blaine had known all along about Daisy's death and his wife's disappearance. He may not be evil like Breanna, but he was responsible. I was about to question him further, but Zach came running over at high speed. "Daddy! You're crying?"

Blaine sniffled. "I'm okay, honey, everything's going to be okay."

Sadie said, "That's right, honey. You and I are going to be okay. You and me, Zachy."

I had a feeling when Sadie said she and her son would be

okay, she was implying Blaine was not part of their future. It was a reasonable assumption, considering he was responsible for the death of a young woman and the unlawful detainment of his wife and child. Blaine Jarreau was going away for a long, long time.

43

HIRSCH

WHEN THE DEA AGENTS ARRIVED, WE SEPARATED SADIE and Blaine. They brought in a dozen agents to assist with the questioning and security of Sadie and her son Zach. Sadie sat in the living room with her son, who happily ate goldfish crackers and drank juice from a sippy cup. Martina sat on the couch next to Sadie, trying to make her feel more comfortable alongside the two DEA agents who questioned her. The agents were careful with their language out of concern for Zach. I was satisfied Sadie was in excellent hands. I headed back to the bedroom where another set of DEA agents were interrogating Blaine.

Before I could reach the room, DEA Agent Pepin pulled me aside. "He's not giving us anything."

"He was talking to us earlier, but then his son ran up, and he wouldn't talk in front of him. He said he knew they had taken a pregnant woman, but things hadn't turned out the way he was expecting. He made it seem like it was all his sister's plan."

"You want another crack at him without the kid around?"

"Don't mind if I do."

I gestured to Martina that I was going to the back room. She nodded in acknowledgment.

We headed down the hallway into a bedroom where Blaine sat cuffed in a big comfy chair. Two agents had brought in chairs from the dining room and sat facing Blaine. One agent stood and offered me his.

After accepting, I situated the chair in front of Blaine. "Blaine, you and I have talked several times in the last month. I believe you truly care for Sadie and for Zach. I even believe that, in some misguided notion, you held them here for their own safety. But here's where this is going to go wrong for you and your family. If you don't tell us everything you know about Breanna and her operation with these babies, and I mean everything, not only will you go to jail for life, but the people Breanna work for could come after you and your family just to keep you quiet. The only way to stop that from happening is to cooperate with us so we can keep them safe and ensure Breanna and her crew are locked up so they won't be free to come after you and your family."

Blaine glanced at the agents and then back at me.

"If I talk, will I get a deal? If I'm locked up, I'm as good as dead."

"You tell us everything you know, everything you took part in, and we'll decide what kind of deal we can make."

Agent Pepin added, "Not only will the sheriff's department work with you, but the DEA can help protect your family. We can only help you if you help us. Based on my experience, if this goes well, we may get you a nice spot in a minimum-security prison, and your wife and child will be safe."

Blaine shook his head in confusion. "I don't understand how the DEA is involved. How can I help you? I don't know anything about any drugs."

Agent Pepin said, "Your sister's mixed up with a Mexican drug lord named Carlos Fuentes. Do you know who that is?"

"I've never heard of him."

"Well, trust me when I say he's a really bad guy. The yacht used to keep the pregnant women hostage belongs to Carlos Fuentes. That is our connection."

What little color Blaine had left drained from his face. My instincts were telling me he did not know a drug lord was involved in the operation. Blaine spoke so quietly it was practically a whisper. "She told me the yacht belonged to an old boyfriend."

I said, "Let's start from the very beginning. Can you do that?"

He was quiet, and I could tell he was contemplating his choices. Either way, his goose was cooked, so he might as well talk.

He nodded. "It was never supposed to be like this. I was out to lunch with Bree..." He recounted the story of meeting Daisy at the restaurant and how she backed out of the deal.

"And then what happened?"

Sweat trickled down Blaine's temple. "About a week after Daisy decided not to give us the baby, Bree called me. She had broken into my boat and said I had to get down to the marina right away. I told her I was working, because I was, and that I wanted her off my boat. She said it was too late for that. At first, I thought it was just typical Bree. Bree did whatever Bree wanted. But then I heard a muffled scream in the background, and I knew she must have done something really awful. I told the staff at the hospital I had an emergency and had another doctor cover my shift. When I arrived at my boat, Bree and an armed man were inside the cabin. They brought me to Daisy — they had her tied up in the stateroom. I told her she had to let Daisy go, and if she didn't, I would call the police. And that's when Bree explained she had a buyer, if I didn't want the baby. She tried to act like it was some kind of gift to Sadie and me."

"Did you know who the buyer was?"

"No."

"What happened next?"

"I told Bree she had lost her mind and if they didn't let Daisy go, I would call the police. That's when Bree threatened to kill me and Sadie if I did. She said that I was complicit because we had already come up with a fake name to adopt the baby illegally and that she would turn me in if I didn't help with the delivery. I should've called the police. I didn't think they would kill Daisy."

Blaine didn't think Breanna would kill the woman they had kidnapped and planned to baby-nap from?

"What happened next?"

"Bree said there was another boat waiting. A yacht that an old boyfriend lent her, where I could deliver the baby when Daisy went into labor. Bree said we could induce to get it over with in the next twenty-four hours. I knew I didn't have any options. So, I went. We took the boat out closer to the Oakland marina, but not near the docks, to make the switch. The yacht was anchored. It was pretty big and already equipped with armed guards."

"And nobody saw this?"

"It was dark, and we weren't near the dock or lights."

"What did the armed guards look like?"

"Hispanic. Dark hair, dark eyes, tall, and well-muscled. Big guns. Not people you would want to mess with."

"What happened when you arrived on the yacht?"

"They brought me into the suite, a birthing suite. It was incredible. They obviously had been planning the operation for a while. After inducement, Daisy delivered a healthy baby early the next morning. Daisy was healthy and recovering. That is when they told me my part was done and that I would be escorted back to my boat. When I got up to leave, I saw Bree walk up to the girl and inject her with something. She started convulsing. I rushed to help her, but Breanna stopped me. She said there couldn't be any witnesses. The baby was taken care of by a female nurse. She washed him, wrapped him up, and fed him a bottle. Daisy didn't even get to hold him."

This man had witnessed the young woman die. He had to feel responsible.

"And that was the first pregnant woman taken?"

"That I know of. You'd have to ask Bree. Considering the setup, I'd be surprised if it wasn't the first."

"And then what? You went home and never spoke of it again?"

"No. She threatened to kill Sadie or me if I ever told. And then she took another pregnant woman and said if I didn't help with the delivery, she would kill Sadie and turn me in and tell the authorities it was all my idea."

"How many more women after Daisy?"

"A lot. And I knew Sadie suspected something was up, with me keeping secrets, being out late at night. It wasn't an affair. It was delivering babies and meeting with Bree."

"You never saw where the babies went?"

He shook his head. "I have no idea. I know they're being sold. I don't know to who. Again, that would be a question for Bree."

"When did you stop?"

"I never stopped."

"We need you to write down the names of all the missing women. All the women who you delivered their babies. If you don't know names, provide descriptions, dates, everything you do know."

"Okay. Their families deserve to know what happened to them."

"And how did Sadie fit in?"

"Wrong place, wrong time. If she were anyone else, she

would be dead. Breanna said Sadie just showed up on the boat. I didn't know she would be there. The guards detained her with one of the pregnant women already on board. She called me and asked me what to do, and I said to let her go. But of course, that wasn't an option. So they brought her to the yacht until we could figure out a plan. After a while, Bree thought Sadie was too much of a liability and wanted to kill her. I didn't want her to do it, but I had no control over it."

"You knew Breanna was going to kill Sadie?"

He nodded. "It was the only way, I guess."

I didn't blame Sadie for wanting to cut Blaine from her life. "But she didn't?"

"Sadie told her she was pregnant. Breanna stopped and called me. She told me Sadie was pregnant, and I couldn't believe it. I didn't believe her. Once her pregnancy was verified, I begged Bree to spare her life. I told her I would make sure Sadie never told anyone about the yacht or the other women. And that we'd come up with a plan. There was no way I could let Bree kill my baby."

But the other women, no problem? "What was the plan for Sadie?"

"I set them up on Orcas Island and gave them new names. Bree insisted on guards. I knew the set-up couldn't last forever, but I was stuck and running out of options. Bree said the people she was working with would kill all of us, including Bree, if we ever went to the police."

"The people were Carlos Fuentes and crew?"

"I guess that makes sense."

"So, all this time, Sadie's been here, and she didn't want to be?"

"It's like she said, I kept her here. She wanted to leave. But it was the only way I could keep them safe. I know she hates me. I can see it in her eyes. I guess I don't blame her."

"Sadie says Breanna shot her?"

"Yes. Sadie was getting more frustrated than usual that she was stuck here, and we got into an argument on one of Breanna's visits. It was an accident. Actually, Bree was threatening us, and I tackled her, and the gun went off. Sadie was hit. Thankfully, she survived. I told Breanna to never come back here, or I would kill her myself."

I glanced over at Agent Pepin. "Is it enough to get Breanna?"

"It is, if he'll testify." Pepin turned to Blaine. "Will you testify?"

"I'll testify if you promise to keep them safe."

"We will."

"Anything else you want to tell us?" I asked.

"I'm sorry."

Right. I stood up and exited the room. Out in the hallway, Agent Pepin said, "Nice work, Detective. What a mess."

"No kidding. I don't even want to think of how many pregnant women have gone missing because of them."

Pepin said, "Thank goodness for that news report."

I said, "It seems to have blown this wide open," and then we discussed the next steps for Sadie and Zach before I walked back into the living room.

Zach had curled up and gone to sleep on the spot next to Sadie. Martina and the agents were across from them. Sadie said, "Don't worry, he's a sound sleeper."

Good. I didn't think a little boy needed to hear any more than he had already. "Blaine told us everything. He is going to cooperate. Also, the DEA will put you into protective custody temporarily. We need to take down some bad people who may want to come after you if they know you planned to testify against them. You'll be in good hands."

"Thank you, Detective and Ms. Monroe. Before I go into protective custody, can I make a few calls?"

Agent Pepin said, "I think that should be fine." He handed Sadie his phone. "You can use mine if you would like."

"Thank you."

Martina got off the sofa and walked over to the corner with me. "Well, I didn't see that coming."

"No." I quickly filled her in on everything Blaine had confessed.

Martina said, "This was definitely one of the stranger cases."

"No kidding."

"Now we need to get Breanna and her goons locked up."

"The DEA is on it."

"I can't wait to get home."

"Me too, but it's pretty late. We could stay over and then head out in the morning. You can't miss Friday night pizza night."

Martina grinned. "No, I cannot."

"Plus, you need plenty of time to prepare for your date on Saturday night," I teased.

"Ugh. Don't remind me."

44

MARTINA

THE BALL SPED DOWN THE LANE AND CRACKED AGAINST one pin, tumbling the others behind it. I'd knocked down four pins. No beginner's luck in my forecast. Dave said, "All right, you're getting better."

Better than a gutter ball, but I wasn't sure I would go beyond that. Dave was nice and not bad looking. He was divorced, never had kids, and worked in finance. I could see why Kim thought we might be friends or more. But the sparks weren't flying, and I doubted there would be a second date. Or maybe I was overthinking the whole thing. Does anybody really fall in love on the first date? I was being too hasty. Except... being on a date with someone new was strange. Too strange. Although it wasn't as bad as I had expected it to be. The conversation had been easy, and we had the whole ex-military thing in common.

"I guess there is hope for me yet."

"Absolutely, Martina Monroe."

I wondered if he liked me or thought I was a catch. I had never thought of myself as a catch. He was a strong, disciplined gentleman. Did most women like that? Not that I didn't, he just wasn't that interesting to me. Or was my bar too high or off completely? It wasn't like we could discuss criminal cases or the best way to take down a suspect. But is that what I really wanted in a life partner? That would be too much of the job, too much of the time. No, I didn't want a clone of myself or even Jared. Maybe something more like Kim and Hirsch had. They balanced each other out. Different but complementary.

Would I know love if I felt it again? With Jared, I felt that heart-pounding rush of adrenaline the first time I met him and couldn't wait to see him whenever we were apart. I knew there would never be another Jared, but as nice as Dave was, I didn't think he was Jared's runner-up either. There was no rush, no desire to see him again. The only desire I felt was for the date to be over.

Dave grabbed his ball and headed up to the lane. With near expert precision, he flung the ball down the lane. Another strike. He was kicking my butt. Had he invited me bowling to show off what a superb athlete he was? Was bowling a sport? Dave returned with a satisfied grin on his face. "You'll get there, don't worry."

As if it was my ambition to become an expert bowler. I had taken down mobsters. Serial killers. Kidnappers. Was he serious? Maybe I was being too sensitive — or he was condescending. Whatever it was about him, it wasn't a fit.

"You up for another game?" he asked.

Was it really fun for him to beat me frame after frame? *No, thank you.* Why would I want to do that again? Just then, my phone buzzed, and out of instinct, I looked and was about to answer. It was rude, and Kim had warned me not to do that when I was on a date because it would give off the signal that I wasn't interested. But, considering...

"I'm sorry, this is my partner. I need to take it."

He looked disappointed, but I answered anyway. "Hey, Hirsch, what's up?"

"Shoot. Sorry. I totally forgot you were on your date. We can talk later."

Uh-huh. He was checking in on me. "Yeah, I'm kinda busy but go ahead, if it's urgent."

"How's it going?"

"Oh, okay, yeah, sure if you can be quick."

I mouthed, sorry, to Dave and stepped away.

Hopefully, Hirsch understood my intonation that I absolutely wanted him to continue. Talking with Hirsch about cases was far more interesting than this guy. I didn't know what happened to him after the Navy or in his life, but maybe looking at numbers all day made him a little, well, boring and out of touch.

Thankfully, I moved far enough away from Dave that he couldn't hear Hirsch's laughter through my phone.

"That good, huh?"

"Yep."

"All right, well, I hate to keep you away from your date too long, but I do have some news."

"What is it?"

"I just got off the phone with the DEA. They have Breanna in custody, and they think she'll flip to save her own butt."

"What does that mean?"

"She's willing to give up Fuentes and his entire organization. She has sensitive information that could help take down the organization."

"Dang."

"The DEA is now busy with Breanna putting together a case to take down Fuentes's drug trafficking operations. He's been operating from Mexico and all along the west coast. Apparently, the baby trafficking was all Breanna's doing. She confirmed fifteen women in total were murdered after giving birth, which matches up with Blaine's list. The babies were sold to wealthy folks from around the world. They do it all in international waters to keep from being detected. After the first few bodies washed up, they started weighting them down. They're putting together dive teams to find them, but it's a big ocean."

Breanna was a serial murderer. She needed to be locked up for the rest of her life. I prayed the DEA ensured a lengthy sentence, even with whatever deal she was going to cut. "How did Breanna get tangled up with Fuentes in the first place?"

"Apparently, she was already part of their drug organization but had suggested the baby scheme when she saw how desperate Blaine and Sadie were to have a baby. She figured if her own brother was desperate enough for a child to do an illegal adoption that there were probably a lot of other folks out there who would too. She was the head of the entire baby-selling operation."

"Please tell me she will not walk on fifteen murders, kidnappings, and illegal sale of children."

"I hope not. It's with the DEA now."

"Does the DEA think they'll be able to find the children?"

"It's too early to tell."

"Thanks for letting me know. Have you talked to Vincent?"

"I talked to him earlier today. He's hanging tight on his suspension. But he's grateful that we could find Sadie, and May is over the moon. Apparently, Amanda was pretty thrilled, and he said he was rewarded — big time. I didn't ask for details."

"Sounds like Vincent."

I glanced over at Dave. He was looking at me as if I had just ruined our entire date. "I should get back."

"Hang in there. If you need me to call back with an emergency, I can."

"No worries, I can handle myself."

"I know you can. Have fun," he said through laughter.

I hung up the phone and returned to my date. "I'm so sorry about that. There was a break in our case this week."

"Sounds like you work a lot."

"I do, but I take time off more than I used to. Zoey's growing up, and I don't want to miss any more of her childhood than I have to."

"She sounds like a great kid."

"She is. And I should probably head home. It's been fun."

"Oh, you don't want to go get a drink?"

If I hadn't killed our date with a work call, I had another trick up my sleeve. I had assumed Kim told him I was in AA, but maybe not. "Kim didn't tell you I'm a recovering alcoholic?"

Dave's face fell. "I'm so sorry. She did. I'm a bonehead."

I wouldn't go that far, but it was a pretty big slip. Not that I was one to talk. "Well, I should get going. The sitter has to be home by a certain time."

Way to think on my feet. *A certain time?* I easily could have said nine or something realistic.

"All right, well, it was nice, Martina."

I nodded and gave him an awkward hug and hurried out of the bowling alley, thankful I had driven myself. Two big accomplishments in one day. One, Breanna was in custody, and two, I survived my first date post-Jared. *Ugh. Those are words I never thought would cross my mind.*

45

MARTINA

Kɪᴍ ᴡᴀs ʀᴀᴅɪᴀɴᴛ ᴀs sʜᴇ ꜰʟᴏᴀᴛᴇᴅ ᴅᴏᴡɴ ᴛʜᴇ ᴀɪsʟᴇ ɪɴ ᴀ fitted silk gown. It was hard to take my eyes off her, but I did just for a moment to glance over at Hirsch, who stood waiting anxiously for his bride. His eyes sparkled, and a grin was plastered on his face. It was the look you would want to see if you were Kim or any other bride heading down the aisle. It was a look of love, excitement, and readiness for the next chapter.

After Kim's father hugged her and shook Hirsch's hand, Kim stepped closer to Hirsch. The two looked like they belonged on top of a wedding cake. A perfect couple. They faced each other, and I took a moment to admire Zoey in her hot pink gown and beaded belt. She wore a crown of pink roses in her hair and a touch of gloss on her lips. My girl was beautiful, inside and out.

Turning to look out at the church, I could tell the guests were as in awe of the couple as I was. Thinking back to my date, I knew Dave wasn't a love match, but that didn't mean there wasn't someone out there for me. Hirsch found love a second time, and Kim had found her perfect match on the first try. The two gave me hope that maybe one day I would be as happy as they were.

After the tear-jerking vows, the happy couple faced their guests as husband and wife. There were cheers and hollers as they triumphantly exited the church. We followed them to the reception hall where there was music and hors d'oeuvres and champagne and non-alcoholic beverages for the children and me.

Kim and her mother had gone all out. It was definitely a festive affair. Lots of sparkle and flowers in pinks and greens and blues. Gorgeous. Zoey ran up to me and held my hand. "Mommy, wasn't that the best wedding ever?"

"It sure was."

"I hope you get married again and I get to be in the wedding. Can I be your maid of honor?" she asked as her blue eyes shone.

Trying my best to keep my emotions in check, I nodded and said, "Absolutely."

"Kim told me that there are sausages wrapped in like a bread, and it's called pigs in a blanket, and I have to try it. She says they are so good, even though they have a silly name. You should try it too."

"I wouldn't miss them." We rarely ate hot dogs in our house, but Zoey loved Kim and hearing about all the details of the wedding. What a day. What a happy, happy day.

Vincent approached in a dark suit and a wide grin. "Ms. Martina Monroe, you look amazing," he said, with a little more surprise than I appreciated.

Amanda, his girlfriend, said, "I second that. You're gorgeous."

Why was everybody so surprised? Sure, I wasn't usually wearing a black fitted gown that had a sparkly belt that matched my 10-year-old daughter's. And yes, even I had put a bit of lipstick on. Zoey and I actually had a lot of fun getting ready for the wedding, but I admit it was a touch dressier than my usual attire of slacks, blouse, and sensible shoes.

"Well, thank you very much."

Zoey added. "Mommy always looks pretty."

My girl.

Amanda smiled. "Yes, she does. And you, my dear, are gorgeous!"

Zoey blushed. "Thank you."

Vincent and I had been reinstated with the CoCo County Sheriff's Department after a one-month suspension. I would be lying if I said that, during that month, I hadn't considered staying with my firm full-time and ending my time with CoCo County. The suspension left an unpleasant taste in my mouth, and I didn't appreciate being punished for doing what I thought was the right thing. As long as LaFontaine was sheriff, I didn't think that type of behavior would change. Also, it had been nice seeing my previous work buddies each day and working with the latest state-of-the-art equipment without too many rules to bind us. It had been a lot like a homecoming of sorts. But after a long conversation with Stavros, we both agreed it was best for the firm and for me if I finished out my contract with the sheriff's department. If there was one positive to my suspension, it was that during my time away, I'd learned Hirsch would always be my friend, or more accurately, my family. There wasn't a single day during that month that we didn't talk, even though we were both working full-time on different cases.

The suspension certainly sent a message to the others but also pointed out that because we had leaked the story to the press not only were the perpetrators of the crime brought to justice, but it also helped bring down an entire drug cartel operating off the coast of California. Sometimes breaking the rules was, in fact, the right thing to do. Don't get me wrong, I was glad to be back working alongside Hirsch and the Cold Case Squad. And I meant what I had said to Hirsch. I wouldn't put our friendship or the squad's future in jeopardy ever again.

Amanda said, "Thank you, again. May is like a different person since Sadie came back. It's such an amazing story."

"Yeah, I certainly didn't predict that one. How are Sadie and Zach doing?" I asked. After the trial and the DEA was certain Sadie and Zach were safe, they could return to the Bay Area. Sadie had already filed for divorce against Blaine and planned to sell their house to buy a new place for her and Zach to start over fresh with their friends and chosen family.

"From what I can tell, they're doing great. Zach just started pre-K, and he loves being at school with the other kids."

"That's so good to hear." And that was why we did this job.

Amanda turned serious. "You know, before Sadie's case, I didn't realize how dangerous your jobs are. And how impactful it can be to reunite families and friends. It's incredible."

I didn't disagree.

Vincent said, "All in a day's work."

Vincent and I had talked a lot during our suspension. He said that as much trouble as the leak had caused him, the fact that it had brought Sadie home, he hadn't regretted it for one second.

Out of the corner of my eye, I spotted Dave. *Ugh, I forgot he would be here.* Our eyes met. "Hi, Dave."

"Oh, hi, Martina. How have you been?"

"I've been well, thank you. You?"

"I've been well. Good to see you." He continued walking.

Ouch. When he was out of earshot, I returned to my group and whispered, "That's the guy I went out with. It didn't end well."

Vincent laughed. "No?"

"It basically ended with Hirsch calling me about the case, and I said I had to go home early. And then he asked me to go to a bar for a drink."

Amanda added, "Not a love match."

"No."

"Well, Kim told me it's a numbers game. Mom, there is someone out there for you. I can feel it in my bones," Zoey said emphatically.

There's that 'Mom' again. I suppose I had better get used to it.

Soon, we were joined by Mom and Sarge and a quick appearance by Dr. Scribner and the rest of the Cold Case Squad. It was such a happy occasion everybody was laughing and smiling. Someone nudged my shoulder, and I turned. "Well, hello, Mr. Man-of-the-hour."

"How did I do?"

"You did amazing, Hirsch. I'm proud of you."

Kim peered out from the other side of Hirsch. "You look stunning, Martina."

"Oh, stop, you're the bride. You're the gorgeous one," I said with a smile.

Hirsch turned to his bride and said, "Yes, I am finding it quite difficult to focus my eyes on anything else."

They exchanged a chaste kiss before returning their attention to the rest of us.

Vincent and Amanda smiled.

Mom said, "Well, it's official. I'm a matchmaker now."

The group laughed.

We partied late into the evening with plenty of cake, snacks, beverages, smiles, laughter, and dancing. It was a magical evening, and I was so grateful to be a part of it. At the end of the night, my feet were sore from dancing, and my face hurt from smiling. We said our goodbyes and headed home. This was definitely one of those memories to keep safe so that when the days were dark, I could pull it out and remember that hope and joy and love existed just beyond the shadows.

THANK YOU!

Thank you for reading *What She Found*. I hope you enjoyed reading it as much as I loved writing it. If you did, I would greatly appreciate if you could post a short review.

Reviews are crucial for any author and can make a huge difference in visibility of current and future works. Reviews allow us to continue doing what we love, *writing stories*. Not to mention, I would be forever grateful!

Thank you!

JOIN H.K. CHRISTIE'S READER CLUB

Join my reader club to be the first to hear about upcoming novels, new releases, giveaways, promotions, as well as, a free e-copy of the **prequel to the Martina Monroe series**, ***Crashing Down.***

It's completely free to sign up and you'll never be spammed by me, you can opt out easily at any time.

Sign up at
www.authorhkchristie.com

The Martina Monroe Series is a nail-biting suspense series starring Private Investigator Martina Monroe. If you like high-stakes games, jaw-dropping twists, and embattled seekers struggling to do right, then you'll love H.K. Christie's thrilling series.

What She Left, Martina Monroe, PI, Book 1

She's on her last chance. When the bodies start piling up, she'll need to save more than her job.

Martina Monroe is a single bad day away from losing it all. Stuck catching insurance fraudsters and cheating spouses due to a DUI, the despondent PI yearns to return to more fulfilling gigs. So when a prospective client asks for her by name to identify an unknown infant in a family photo, she leaps at the opportunity and travels to the one place she swore never to go: back home.

As the pressure mounts and the temptation of booze calls like a siren, Martina digs into the mystery and discovers many of the threads have razor-sharp ends. And forced to partner with a resentful detective investigating a linked suspicious death, the haunted private eye unravels clues that delve deep into her past... and put her in a dark and dangerous corner.

Can this gritty detective unlock the truth before she's drowned in a sea of secrets?

If She Ran, Martina Monroe, PI, Book 2

Three months. Three missing women. One PI

determined to discover the truth.

Back from break, PI Martina Monroe clears the air with her boss at Drakos Security & Investigations and is ready to jump right into solving cold cases for the CoCo County Sheriff's Department.

Diving into the cold case files Martina stumbles upon a pattern of missing young women, all of whom were deemed runaways, and the files froze with minimal detective work from the original investigators. The more Martina digs into the women's last days the more shocking discoveries she makes.

Soon, Martina and Detective Hirsch not only uncover additional missing women but when their star witness turns up dead, they must rush to the next before it's too late.

A gripping, unputdownable thriller full of mystery and suspense.

All She Wanted, Martina Monroe, PI, Book 3

A tragic death. A massive cover-up. PI Martina Monroe must face her past in order to reveal the truth.

PI Martina Monroe has found her groove working cold cases alongside Detective Hirsch at the CoCo County Sheriff's Department. With a growing team of cold case detectives, Martina and Hirsch are on the heels of bringing justice for Julie DeSoto - a woman Martina failed to protect one year earlier. But when Martina receives a haunting request from her past, it nearly tears her in two.

As Julie's case turns hot, so does the investigation into a young soldier's untimely death. As both cases rattle Martina to the core, she now questions everything she believed about her time working for Drakos Security & Investigations and with the United States Army. Martina must uncover the truth for her sanity and her own life.

Pushed to the brink, Martina risks everything to expose the real criminals and bring justice for the victim's family and her own.

A gripping, page-turning thriller, full of suspense.

Why She Lied, Martina Monroe, PI, Book 4

A missing mother and child. A secret past revealed. Will Martina and Hirsch discover the truth before they meet their end?

In the thick of the current cold case investigation, PI Martina Monroe receives a hand-written letter from a desperate mother pleading for Martina and Hirsch to reopen the cold case of the woman's missing daughter and five-year-old grandson. Feeling a deep connection to the request, Martina knows that Hirsch and she have found their next case.

As the two investigators dig into the life of Ana and her son, Ryder, they quickly find Ana has the life many would be envious of. With a loving group of family and friends, a devoted husband, and a successful career, Ana's perfect life seems a bit too perfect for Martina and Hirsch.

Searching even further into Ana's past, they find a startling secret that leads Martina and Hirsch into the dark world of organized crime. Hot on the trail, the two investigators head to New York City, hoping to find the answer to what happened to Ana and Ryder. However, as soon as they touch down, they realize they aren't the only ones on the hunt.

Will Martina and Hirsch discover the truth before they become victims themselves?

Secrets She Kept, Martina Monroe, PI, Book 5

A ritualistic murder. Multiple suspects. Can the cold

case detectives find the truth before the killers strike again?

Ten years earlier, two teenage girls were found murdered by what appeared to be a satanic sacrifice. The case had dominated the news headlines for months before the original investigators failed to arrest the perpetrators of the crime - despite multiple suspects. Without solid evidence to prosecute, and even with the near-heroic efforts of the original detectives, the homicide investigation turned cold. For years, the families of the two victims fought to keep the young women's memory alive and to get the attention of law enforcement to not give up on finding those responsible.

In an election year, and with a stellar record for the CoCo County Sheriff's Department Cold Case Squad, the Sheriff hands cold case investigators Martina Monroe and Detective Hirsch the most notorious decade-old murder case - named by the press, 'The Twin Satan Murders.' Unlike most of their previous cold cases, The Twin Satan Murders were thoroughly investigated by previous detectives. Undeterred by the lack of evidence and answers from the original investigation, Martina and Hirsch investigate the murders as if it were day one.

Knocking on doors, Martina and Hirsch are surprised by the lack of cooperation from the original witnesses. With pushback from the community, the two investigators are forced to dive into the world of the occult. What the two detectives find is more disturbing than any case they've worked on before. Soon, Martina and Detective Hirsch find that some powerful people will go to all lengths to keep the truth buried.

Will Martina and Detective Hirsch find the actual killers before they become victims themselves?

The Selena Bailey Series is a suspenseful series featuring a young Selena Bailey and her turbulent path to becoming a top notch kick-ass private investigator as led by her mentor, Martina Monroe.

Not Like Her, Selena Bailey, Book 1

A battered mother. A possessive boyfriend. Can she save herself from a similar fate?

Selena longs to flee her uneasy home life. Prepping every spare minute for a college escape, the headstrong, high school senior vows never to be like her alcoholic mom with her string of abusive boyfriends. So when Selena finds her beaten nearly to death, she knows safety is slipping away...

With her mother's violent lover evading justice, Selena's new boyfriend's offer to move in seems Heaven-sent. But jealous rage and a renewed search for her long-lost father threaten to pull her back into harm's way.

Can Selena break free of an ugly past, or will brutal men crush her hopes of a better future?

Not Like Her is the first book in the suspenseful Selena Bailey series. If you like thrilling twists, dark tension, and smart and driven women, then you'll love H.K. Christie's new dark mystery series.

Trigger warning: This book includes themes relating to domestic violence

---

One In Five, Selena Bailey, Book 2

A predator running free and the girl determined to stop him.

After escaping a violent past, Selena Bailey, starts her first semester of college determined to put it all behind her - until her roommate is attacked at the Delta Kappa Alpha house. After reporting the attack, police refuse to prosecute due to lack of evidence, claiming another case of 'he said, she said'.

As Selena and Dee begin meeting other victims, it's clear Dee's assault wasn't an isolated event. Selena determined to take down the DKA house, takes matters into her own hands in order to claim justice for Dee and prevent the next attack.

Will Selena get justice for the women of SFU or will she become the next victim?

On The Rise, Selena Bailey, Book 3

A little girl is taken. A mysterious cover-up. One young investigator determined to find the truth.

Selena Bailey, a sophomore at the local university studying criminal justice, returns from winter break to jump into her first official case as a private investigator with her stepmother's security firm.

Thrown into an undercover detail, Selena soon discovers a much darker plot. What seemed like a tragic kidnapping is revealed to be just the tip of the iceberg. Will Selena expose the truth before not only the little girl's life, but her own is lost forever?

Go With Grace, Selena Bailey, Book 4

A dangerous stalker. A desperate classmate. Will one young investigator risk everything to help a stranger in need?

Selena Bailey returns in her senior year of college determined to keep her head down and out of other people's lives with the sole intent of keeping them safe and out of harm's way.

Selena is focused more than ever, with three major goals: graduate with her bachelor's degree in Criminal Justice, obtain her Private Investigator's license and find her late boyfriend, Brendon's, killers.

Her plans are derailed when a desperate classmate approaches Selena for her help. At first, she refuses but Dillon is certain his life is in danger and provides Selena with proof. With no one else to turn to, Selena reluctantly takes the case.

The investigation escalates quickly as Selena soon discovers the woman stalking Dillon is watching his, and now Selena's, every move.

Will Selena be able to save Dillon's life and her own?

Flawless, Selena Bailey, Book 5

A young woman clinging on to life. A desperate family fighting for answers. Will Selena be able to discover the truth in time to save her?

Selena Bailey returns with her Private Investigator license in one hand and the first official case for Bailey Investigations in the other.

When the sister of a young woman, fighting for her life in the Intensive Care Unit, pleads with Selena to explore her sister, Stephanie's, last days before she slipped into a coma, Selena must go undercover in the billion dollar beauty industry to discover the truth.

The deeper Selena delves into Stephanie's world, the more she fears for Stephanie's life and so many others.

As Selena unravels the truth behind an experimental weight loss regimen, she finds it's not only weight the good doctor's patients are losing. Selena now must rush against the clock to save not only Stephanie's life, but her own.

A Permanent Mark: A heartless killer. Weeks without answers. Can she move on when a murderer walks free?

Kendall Murphy's life comes crashing to a halt at the news her husband has been killed in a tragic hit-and-run. Devastated and out-of-sorts, she can't seem to come to terms with the senselessness of it all. Despite, promises by a young detective, she fears they'll never find the person responsible for her husband's death.

As months go by without answers, Kendall, with the help of her grandmother and sister, deals with her grief as she tries to create a new life for herself. But when the detective discovers that the death was a murder-for-hire, suddenly everyone from her new love interest and those closest to her are under suspicion. And it may only be a matter of time before the assassin strikes again...

Can Kendall trust anyone, or will misplaced loyalty make her the next victim?

If you like riveting suspense and gripping mysteries then you'll love *A Permanent Mark* - starring a grown up Selena Bailey.

ABOUT THE AUTHOR

H. K. Christie watched horror films far too early in life. Inspired by the likes of Stephen King, true crime podcasts, and a vivid imagination she now writes suspenseful thrillers featuring unbreakable women. *Secrets She Kept* is her 16th published book.

When not working on her latest novel, she can be found eating & drinking with friends, walking around the lakes, or playing with her favorite furry pal.

She is a native and current resident of the San Francisco Bay Area.

www.authorhkchristie.com

ACKNOWLEDGMENTS

Part of the inspiration for *What She Found* came from the recent surge in documentary and press around the Lacy Peterson murder in 2002. In contrast, a few members of the press pointed out at the lack of press coverage of a missing pregnant woman and her five-year old son, Evelyn and Alexis Hernandez, just seven months before Lacy Peterson disappeared. Evelyn's body was found a month later in the San Francisco Bay, but her son, Alexis was never found. Do you remember that press coverage? Neither do I - and at the time I lived in the San Francisco Bay Area and even worked just a few miles from the waters where the women's bodies were found. Why did one woman get more press coverage than the other? I think these are questions we need to ask more often - so I had my pals Martina and Hirsch do just that in *What She Found*.

And yes, I think of Martina and Hirsch as real people - they just happened to live in my brain.

And... I extend my deepest gratitude to my Advanced Reader Team. My ARC Team is invaluable in taking the first look at my stories and spreading awareness of my stories through their reviews and kind words.

To my editor Paula Lester, a huge thank you for your careful edits and helpful comments. And many thanks to my proof reader, Becky Stewart.

To my cover designer, Odile, thank you for your guidance and talent.

Last but not least, I'd like to thank all of my readers. It's because of you I'm able to continue doing what I love - writing stories.

Made in United States
North Haven, CT
14 October 2022